BUZZ AROUND THE TRACK

They Said It…

"I'm running a successful business, raising three kids and recovering from my family's latest tragedy. The last thing I need in my life is a playboy race car driver like Garrett Clark. No matter how good he looks."
—Grace Hunt Winters

"Racing is my life. My affairs with women are just a way to blow off steam. Except for Grace. She's different. She makes me want things I never knew I could have."
—Garrett Clark

"We know who sent those anonymous tips about our baby girl. We know where our missing daughter is. Now we just have to tell her the truth about her identity."
—Patsy Grosso

"Our daughter is not the infant we lost, she's a grown woman with a life of her own. Learning the truth…it's going to be hard. We'll welcome her with open arms and give her all the time she needs."
—Dean Grosso

JEAN BRASHEAR

A three-time RITA® Award finalist, *RT Book Reviews* Series Storyteller of the Year and recipient of numerous other awards, Jean has always enjoyed the chance to learn something new while doing research for her books—but never has any subject swept her off her feet like NASCAR. Starting out as someone who wondered what could possibly be interesting about cars driving around a track, she's become a die-hard fan, only too happy to tell anyone she meets how fascinating the world of NASCAR is. For pictures of her racing adventures, visit www.jeanbrashear.com.

NASCAR

CROSSING THE LINE

Jean Brashear

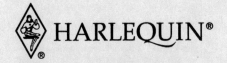

HARLEQUIN®

TORONTO • NEW YORK • LONDON
AMSTERDAM • PARIS • SYDNEY • HAMBURG
STOCKHOLM • ATHENS • TOKYO • MILAN • MADRID
PRAGUE • WARSAW • BUDAPEST • AUCKLAND

Recycling programs
for this product may
not exist in your area.

ISBN-13: 978-0-373-18534-4

CROSSING THE LINE

Copyright © 2010 by Harlequin Books S.A.

Jean Brashear is acknowledged as the author of this work.

NASCAR® and the NASCAR Library Collection® are registered trademarks of the National Association for Stock Car Auto Racing, Inc.

This edition published by arrangement with Harlequin Books S.A.

® and TM are trademarks of the publisher. Trademarks indicated with ® are registered in the United States Patent and Trademark Office, the Canadian Trade Marks Office and in other countries.

www.eHarlequin.com

Printed in U.S.A.

In memory of Matt Barbini, chef and ice sculptor extraordinaire,
and with best wishes to his
courageous and charming parents, Dennis and Frances

ACKNOWLEDGMENTS

To the gang on the eHarlequin NASCAR forum, especially Kat,
Papaya, crazyfor24, Jo Ann from Australia, Miss Jo, Val, Susan,
Tammy and moderator Wayne—thanks for the fun!

To Heather Newton for keeping at least a zillion details straight
as this series enters its third year—
you are amazing!

To Marsha Zinberg, Stacy Boyd and Karen Reid
for the sheer fun of working with you,
as well as the honor of being part of this.

And, as always, to my beloved Ercel,
who hasn't yet run screaming from just one more NASCAR factoid.

NASCAR HIDDEN LEGACIES

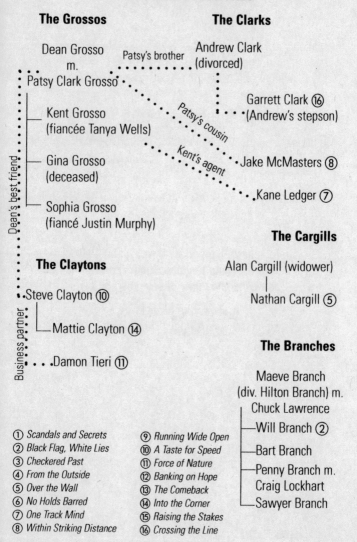

The Grossos

Dean Grosso
m.
Patsy Clark Grosso

— Kent Grosso
(fiancée Tanya Wells)

— Gina Grosso
(deceased)

— Sophia Grosso
(fiancé Justin Murphy)

Patsy's brother

The Clarks

Andrew Clark
(divorced)

Garrett Clark ⑯
(Andrew's stepson)

Patsy's cousin

Kent's agent

Jake McMasters ⑧

Kane Ledger ⑦

Dean's best friend

The Claytons

Steve Clayton ⑩

— Mattie Clayton ⑭

Damon Tieri ⑪

Business partner

The Cargills

Alan Cargill (widower)

Nathan Cargill ⑤

The Branches

Maeve Branch
(div. Hilton Branch) m.
Chuck Lawrence

— Will Branch ②

— Bart Branch

— Penny Branch m.
Craig Lockhart

— Sawyer Branch

① *Scandals and Secrets*
② *Black Flag, White Lies*
③ *Checkered Past*
④ *From the Outside*
⑤ *Over the Wall*
⑥ *No Holds Barred*
⑦ *One Track Mind*
⑧ *Within Striking Distance*
⑨ *Running Wide Open*
⑩ *A Taste for Speed*
⑪ *Force of Nature*
⑫ *Banking on Hope*
⑬ *The Comeback*
⑭ *Into the Corner*
⑮ *Raising the Stakes*
⑯ *Crossing the Line*

THE FAMILIES AND THE CONNECTIONS

The Sanfords

Bobby Sanford
(deceased)
m.
Kath Sanford

— Adam Sanford ①

— Brent Sanford ⑫

— Trey Sanford ⑨

The Hunts

Dan Hunt
m.
Linda (Willard) Hunt
(deceased)

— Ethan Hunt ⑥

— Jared Hunt ⑮

— Hope Hunt ⑫

— Grace Hunt Winters ⑯
(widow of Todd Winters)

The Mathesons

Brady Matheson
(widower)
(fiancée Julie-Anne Blake)

— Chad Matheson ③

— Zack Matheson ⑬

— Trent Matheson
(fiancée Kelly Greenwood)

The Daltons

Buddy Dalton
m.
Shirley Dalton

— Mallory Dalton ④

— Tara Dalton ①

— Emma-Lee Dalton

CHAPTER ONE

"MOMMY."

As Grace Winters concentrated on rolling out pastry for her famous pecan tassies, her middle child Millie's soft voice didn't register at first. Grace had a pastry chef now, but Sarah had disappeared. The celebrity luncheon Gourmet by Grace was catering would begin in two hours; there was no time to waste.

"What, sweetie?" She didn't normally take her children on the job, but since their father's untimely death in an accident two years ago, Millie was still fragile. Grace felt better if they were with family when they couldn't be with her. Today was a school holiday, and her father had a doctor's appointment. Her sister, Hope, was due to pick them up anytime.

"Grace, can you come here?" shouted one of the line cooks.

"Just a second, honey." Grace placed one hand on six-year-old Millie's head. "Can it wait, Al?"

"Only if you don't care that the fish guy didn't deliver enough salmon."

Grace squeezed her eyes shut. "Where's Barbini?" Her new executive chef was already a godsend, but the staff and suppliers still had a bad habit of consulting her first.

"I'm here, Grace," said a quiet, deep voice. "I'm on it."

"Thank you." Barbini's steadiness was the polar opposite of her partner—make that ex-partner—and brother-in-law Tony. Grace still had anxious moments remembering when he'd held a gun on her in the confrontation when he'd admitted to killing team owner Alan Cargill—and embezzling from her, to boot. While she'd been stretched thin and sleeping barely four hours a night trying to shore up the company's bottom line, Tony had been skimming money even faster. Finding out he'd committed a murder, as well…she still couldn't absorb it. Tony was in jail and unlikely to leave, and she was trying to pick up the pieces.

"Mom!" called out her son, Matthew. "Bella just wrote all over my drawing!"

Dear heaven, if Hope didn't show up soon to pick up the kids, she didn't know what she'd do.

"I'm coming!" She grasped Millie's hand and walked quickly through the mayhem of the kitchen in full throttle. "Where's Sarah?" she asked Al. "She should be mixing the filling already."

"Dunno." He shrugged, extending the phone toward Barbini. "Haven't seen her in a while."

"Mommy—"

"Just a second, honey. You're okay, right?" Grace scanned Millie, the child who'd taken Todd's death the hardest, for signs of injury. "You're not hurt?"

Millie's hair, mink-brown like Todd's, swung as she shook her head.

Relieved that Millie was not, as often happened, hiding in the closet, Grace towed her along as she went in search of her other two. "Good. Sweetheart, Aunt Hope will be here very soon. If you can just wait a second until I see what Bella—"

"But I know where Sarah is, Mommy."

Grace whirled. "You do? Where?"

Millie nodded and pointed toward the utility closet about fifteen feet away.

"Why would Sarah be in the closet?"

Millie ducked her head and dug one toe of her shoe into the floor, mumbling.

"Honey," Grace said, kneeling before her child and gently lifting her chin, "I need you to speak up."

"Kissing," Millie said softly. "She's kissing a man."

"When we have an event in two hours?" Grace shot to her feet, forgetting how they were aching. In a few long strides, she reached the door. Surely even Sarah wouldn't—

Grace wrenched the door open, and two people tumbled out. "Grace, I…" Sarah brushed at her tousled hair and made a futile attempt to straighten her clothes.

Sarah was an airhead in real life but a dream in the kitchen. Grace had hoped to groom her to move up, but she had just reached her limit in tolerating Sarah's irresponsible behavior. "Get back to work," she said, her jaw locked tight enough to crack teeth. "You and I will talk later."

Sarah skittered past, and Grace focused for the first time on the amused brown eyes of the too-handsome man in front of her, his own dark hair tumbling over his forehead as it often did in the posters that many a female NASCAR fan had up on her wall.

"You," she said flatly. "What are you doing in my kitchen?" She didn't know Garrett Clark well, but it was impossible not to know of him if you had anything to do with NASCAR. Even if her dad hadn't been a former crew chief, with a NASCAR-themed cookbook due to debut at Daytona and being the caterer of choice for the teams, she had more than a little involvement in the sport.

The driver of the No. 402 FastMax Racing car was, in her opinion, the worst of the worst, a born maverick who cared about nothing but racing and left a trail of broken hearts behind him at every track.

"Something smells real good in here. Mind if I have a taste?" He grinned at her as if nothing had happened. As though he had the right to just stroll in wherever he wanted.

"You'll get your taste at the luncheon. Get out of my kitchen." She turned away, then back. "And leave my staff alone."

"Hey, she dragged me in there." He lifted his palms and looked cat-in-cream cool. "What's a red-blooded guy to do?"

"You—" Suddenly all that was wrong in her life rolled over her like an avalanche, and she was drowning in responsibilities and worries and loneliness and—

Grace felt her vision narrowing, her knees growing weak. She could hear Millie whimper, and she reached out for her poor, suffering child, but she couldn't seem to touch her and the room was spinning and…

The last thing she heard was shouting.

GARRETT CLARK HAD NEVER appreciated his fast reflexes more than when he managed to catch the curvaceous blonde before she hit the floor.

Once he had her in his arms, though, all hell broke loose. The little girl was wailing, the cupcake who'd lured him into the closet was shrieking and somebody dropped a huge pan with a clang.

Then a tornado of a boy, dark and unsmiling, tore through the gathering crowd. "What did you do to my mom?"

A driver had to be able to keep a cool head under any kind of pressure, and Garrett was better at that than most. "Call nine-one-one," he barked at one of the staff. "Your mom just fainted," he said to the boy. *I hope.* He felt for a pulse at her throat, relieved to discover one, even if it seemed too fast to him.

"See to your sister," he ordered, nodding at the little girl who'd discovered him in the closet with the cupcake. "She's scared." Then he lowered his voice a notch and addressed the girl directly. "She's going to be okay, honey." Though he actually had no idea if that were the case. For all he knew, the blonde had stroked out, she'd been so furious.

He returned his attention to the woman in his arms. "Grace." They'd never exactly been introduced, but it was hard to be around NASCAR these days and not know who she was. "Come on, babe. Wake up." There were shadows beneath her eyes, and though she possessed impressive curves, he could feel her ribs beneath his hand. She looked worn-out.

Then EMS was there, and he gratefully relinquished custody.

"I suggest you leave now," said a man in chef's garb.

The guy's tone got Garrett's back up. "I'll leave when I'm ready." Though he had no idea why he would want to stay. He was due for a meeting with his crew chief, and it wasn't going to be pretty. The pressures of this season, three races from the end, were getting to everyone.

Which was why the respite of a few minutes flirting with the pretty Sarah had been appealing.

The man's eyes narrowed. "Have you had a look at those kids? Their father is gone, their mother is working herself half to death, and their uncle held her at gunpoint, then confessed to murder as well as to stealing her money. Now the only parent they have left collapsed in front of them, all because you have no self-discipline."

You have no self-discipline, Garrett, his stepfather and team owner had accused him just last night. *You go off half-cocked, so damn sure you're right. You're going to cost us the championship.*

Stung, Garrett opened his mouth to fire back, but just then, he caught sight of Grace's daughter standing just behind the paramedics, grungy stuffed rabbit clasped tightly in her arms, her brown eyes wide with terror.

He knew nothing about raising kids, but he knew a lot about being small and scared. He took a step toward her, just as the man's arm shot out to block him. Before he could brush it aside, a distraught young woman reached the little girl.

"Millie, come with me, sweetheart."

"Aunt Hope, Mom collapsed. Is she—" The boy who'd raced to his mother's rescue so fiercely looked anything but fierce now.

"She's in the best of hands, sweetheart," the woman assured him. "Where's Bella?"

Garrett watched as the younger woman gathered up

Grace's children and followed the gurney outside. Grace was lying too still, and he found himself wanting to follow.

"All right, everyone," said the man by his side. "We can't help Grace by screwing up this luncheon. Back to work."

The gathered crowd scurried off to their stations, but the chef was obviously waiting for Garrett to leave.

Their uncle held her at gunpoint, then confessed to murder. Holy crap. Tony Winters. The news was all over NASCAR that deceased team owner Alan Cargill's murderer had been caught at last. "I'm sorry, man. I didn't think about the connection. Were they close?"

The chef snorted. "She trusted him, he was her partner, and he was stealing from her to pay gambling debts. You tell me."

Wow. No wonder the woman was so stressed out. "I'm going to the hospital." He might not know Grace personally, but basic decency required that he not simply walk away.

"Just leave her alone. She's got more than she can handle already." The man glowered. "And she's not one of your bimbos." He shot a glare at cupcake Sarah.

Garrett would have laughed at the very notion—no one could be further from his type than a mother of three—but laughter was very much out of place in this situation. And popping this jerk in the mouth would not endear him to anyone, his team owner, his crew chief or NASCAR. This close to the end of the season, he could only afford a laser focus on one thing: racing. Andrew Clark had bet all the marbles on Garrett winning the championship, and if he screwed up, he could take the entire FastMax Racing organization down with him.

He'd never dreamed that a chivalrous impulse to escort the girl he'd met in a club last night to her job this morning could go so awry. He'd only been blowing off steam at the club as a way to deal with the mounting pressures, but he'd never intended to hurt anyone.

"I've got a meeting." Before he could get himself in trouble and jeopardize everything, Garrett forced himself not to respond to the man's insult but simply to walk away.

He'd check on her, this woman he'd wronged, however unintentionally, to be sure she was okay.

Then he'd put her out of his mind and focus on the only thing that could matter right now: proving that a dark horse, a maverick who didn't play the game, could beat the better-funded, fat-cat teams like the Grossos and Sanfords who were heavily favored to win.

He had to put it all on the line for one thing and one thing only: giving the man who'd believed in him, who'd kept him when his own mother had moved on, the championship Andrew Clark had waited years to claim.

CHAPTER TWO

"HOPE, I DON'T HAVE TIME for this," Grace said from the sofa where four-year-old Bella was tenderly, if awkwardly, tucking an afghan around her neck. "I have bills to pay and a proposal to write for the Mason wedding, plus Matthew's end-of-season soccer party is in two weeks."

"The doctor said you should rest," her sister replied as she walked in from the kitchen. "One evening won't kill you."

"You have no idea—" Just then, the doorbell rang.

"I'll get it! I bet it's Grandpop!" cried Bella. She raced to the front door.

The front door wasn't visible from Grace's perch on the sofa, but Grace was surprised that her father had rung the bell. Or that he'd come to the front, for that matter. Her house was generally filled with the chaos of her children and their friends, her siblings and assorted dates or spouses, her friends and neighbors—no one she knew ever did more than a perfunctory knock on the kitchen door off the driveway before walking inside. Coming from a large mixed family of step and half siblings, with a husband whose family had grown up next door to her own childhood home, Grace did not stand on ceremony. People just had to get used to seeing her in her bathrobe or pj's if they came at the wrong time.

"Daddy? Come on in. Tell Hope to go away," Grace called out.

"Don't you dare, Daddy," said Hope, drying her hands on a dish towel.

Both fell silent as Bella returned, beaming as she held the hand of someone much younger than Dan Hunt, displaying him as though he were a great prize she'd been given. "Look, Mommy. Flowers!"

Garrett Clark. Possibly the last person on earth Grace wanted to see right now.

Just then, Matthew skidded into the room. "What are you doing here?" His face was his father's at Todd's most intimidating, revealing the man this skinny eight-year-old would become.

"Matthew," Grace snapped. "Mind your manners. Mr. Clark is a guest in our home," she said more gently. "For the moment," she continued, a warning in her tone. Manners were manners, whatever she might feel about Garrett Clark.

"But it's his fault—"

"It is." There was no lazy laughter in the brown eyes now. "But I wanted to come see for myself that your mother's okay now," Garrett said. "First, though, is Millie here?"

Grace's eyes went wide, but Matthew spoke first. "What do you want with my sister?" He turned to Bella. "Why are you holding his hand?"

"He's pretty," said Bella simply.

Grace heard Hope snort behind her and had a hard time resisting chuckling herself. Bella had an affection for anything she considered pretty. She was a girlie-girl who'd subject anyone not fast enough with an excuse to endless hours of trying clothes on dolls or putting on pretend makeup or playing dress-up.

"I came to apologize." Garrett's expression was somewhere between embarrassed and appalled. "Anyway, guys can't be pretty."

Grace thought a lot of people would be amused by Mr. Charming and Cocky being so off-kilter. She decided to spare him and threw off the afghan, then rose.

"Whoa, there," Garrett said. "Shouldn't you be in bed?"

"Please," Grace replied with a shake of her head. "Not

you, too. I'm far from helpless." And to prove it, she took the reins of her life again. "Bella, honey, go get Millie. Matthew, is your homework done?" She turned to her sister. "Hope, don't you have dinner plans with Brent?" She was tired, heavens yes, but that was simply her life. Too many people depended on her to remain in control. "Are those for me?" She nodded toward the massive bouquet in Garrett's hands.

"Oh—yeah." He thrust them toward her and nearly bobbled the vase as he tried to transfer his other package to one hand.

It was a unicorn, a stuffed one. Grace lifted her eyes in a question.

"This one's not for you. It's for Millie. I heard about, uh—" He flushed a little. "Sarah explained about the closets."

"Sarah," Grace said darkly.

"Listen, what happened was all a big mistake."

"It certainly was."

"No, I mean—" But before he could finish, Millie followed Bella into the living room, her chin tucked near her chest, her ancient bunny clasped to her side.

"Millie, Mr. Clark is here to see you."

Shyly, Millie raised the blue eyes that were the only sign she was Grace's child. Otherwise, she, like Matthew, strongly resembled their father. Only Bella had inherited Grace's blond hair.

Grace had to admit to being impressed that Garrett dropped to a crouch before Millie, bringing his eyes to her level. "I'm sorry I invaded your closet," he said. "And I'm sorry your mother fainted." His tone turned casual. "This fellow was in the hospital gift shop, and he kept asking me to bring him to Millie. I wonder if you would be willing to keep him?"

"I will," Bella answered first. "He's pretty."

Garrett's eyes lit with amusement. "I bet you would, and if I'd known I'd meet you, I would have listened harder to see if anyone else in that shop was asking to come to see you."

"You could go back there," Bella said, tilting her head in the flirtatious manner that had been hers from birth.

Garrett laughed out loud then. "I might have to." He turned back to Millie. "But how about you, Miss Millie? You gonna make this guy go home with me? He didn't like it when I tried to feed him nachos."

Millie's lips curved then. "Unicorns don't eat nachos," she said softly.

"See there," Garrett responded. "I knew you'd be the right one to take care of him. You already know more about feeding him than I do." He held the unicorn out to her.

Millie's gaze cut to Grace. "Is it okay, Mommy?" Both hesitation and hope shone in her eyes.

"Of course." Grace looked at him. "And thank you for my flowers. They're lovely." They were a surprise, actually, a unique arrangement of exotic blooms like bird-of-paradise, anthurium and ginger. She'd have pegged him for a typical playboy bachelor choice like roses—not that she had any personal experience with bachelors since Todd had died. She barely had time to take a shower, much less go out on a date. Even if she were ready—which was still uncertain.

Slowly Millie took the unicorn from his hand and brought it close to her face, whispering something into the unicorn's ear. Then she listened intently for long seconds and finally smiled. Her face was brighter than Grace had seen it in a long time when she looked back at Garrett. "He says he's a she, and her name is Seraphina."

"Uh, that's great, uh—" The confusion and uncertainty on Garrett's face were both comical and surprising. He cast Grace a quick glance as if to ask what he should do next, but then he switched his attention right back to Millie before Grace could respond. "See, I told you—it's obvious you're exactly the right person for him—um, her." He shrugged comically. "I mean, when a person can't even tell that a unicorn's a she and not a he, well…I have to go to the experts. Thank you, Miss Millie. It's a comfort to know Seraphina's in the right hands."

Millie stood a little straighter at the praise, and Grace reconsidered some of the blacker thoughts she'd had about Garrett Clark. Millie had been so lost since Todd died, despite grief counseling and the devotion of every single relative. If this man could make Millie feel proud and strong, even for a few minutes, that counted for something with Grace.

Then he looked at Matthew. "Sorry, sport. I should have brought something for you, too—wait." He pulled his sunglasses from his shirt pocket—Oakley glasses, expensive as the earth, for heaven's sake—and put them on Matthew.

Before she could register a protest, they promptly slid right down her son's nose.

"Oh—guess that's not…" Then he brightened. "I have a brand-new design No. 402 car cap in my car. Want it?"

Despite his earlier skepticism about the man, her son's gaze lit. He had a former crew chief for a grandfather, a current one for an uncle and a genius engine builder for another uncle. His father's family might not be much on racing, but Grace's own had been raised around the track. "Well, my uncle Ethan might not like me wearing a FastMax cap instead of one for Sanford Racing." Matthew was loyal to a fault.

"Yeah, I get that." Garrett's forehead wrinkled. "You like video games?"

"Yeah!" Then Matthew's gaze cut to Grace. "That is, I've tried a few, but my mom says we need to play outside and read and stuff."

"One of those, huh?" Garrett lost every last point he'd gained when he leaned closer to her son and sighed. "Moms are like that, I guess."

Then he caught a glimpse of the displeasure she didn't trouble to hide. "Well…" He rose. "I guess I'd better go."

"No!" Bella protested.

Millie sidled a little closer to him.

Even Matthew appeared conflicted.

And Grace grew tired all over again. "Tonight isn't—"

"Grace needs to rest." Hope, bless her, intervened, and this time Grace didn't quarrel. "Mr. Clark understands that, I'm sure." Her background as a psychologist made Hope smooth as silk at maneuvering people. "I'll see you out."

He frowned, but he didn't argue. "I'll think of something," he promised Matthew, then turned to Bella. "And I'll be listening for your name to be called out. Bye, Millie."

"Bye," she said softly.

"What do you say?" Grace asked.

"Thank you."

"You're welcome." He looked at Grace. "Listen, I'm—"

"It was nothing," Grace responded, losing steam by the second. Then she roused herself. "But stay out of my catering kitchen," she called after him as Hope ushered him out the door.

"He's pretty, Mommy," Bella repeated.

He is, Grace thought. *And trouble with a capital* T. *Goodbye and good riddance.*

"WHERE THE HELL HAVE you been?" barked Robbie Smith, Garrett's crew chief, the instant he walked into the race shop.

"Good evening to you, too. Glad to see you're in a great mood, as usual."

"I'll be Little Mary Sunshine after we win the championship, not until." Robbie, a short, squat fireplug of a man, had forgotten more about racing than half the garage had ever learned.

Which was why Andrew Clark, Garrett's dad—stepdad, actually, though Andrew had proved more reliable by far than Garrett's own mother—and team owner had hired the man who intimidated even him a little, and Andrew was no pushover.

He was, though, a very determined man. Andrew had been a poor relation to racing's royalty, the Grosso clan, ever since his sister Patsy had married into the family years ago. Andrew and Patsy were close but also competitive. Patsy wasn't just the wife and mother of champions—she had the instinct to win herself, which was why she was her husband Dean's full partner in their new team, Cargill-Grosso Racing, now that she'd convinced Dean to hang up his driving gloves and become an owner.

Too bad their first year had been marred by the continuing drama of the mystery blogger who insisted that the baby girl—twin to their son Kent—who'd been kidnapped as an infant, had not died as they'd been told but had instead grown up to become part of NASCAR herself.

The knowledge that the child she'd never been able to give up on might be out there somewhere, thirty years later—and might even be someone Patsy knew—was taking its toll on her. The line of would-be Ginas stretched around the block, sort of like all the girls in Cinderella hoping to fit the glass slipper.

And meanwhile, his aunt and uncle—if only by marriage—bled a little every day. He admired them both and would be very glad for their sake when the mystery was unraveled.

"Did you hear me?" Robbie growled. "Get your head out of the clouds, or off whatever woman whose bed you just rolled out of, and come study this engine data."

Garrett could almost laugh at Robbie's assumption. Grace Hunt Winters might have been lying down when he arrived, but if he'd made one move toward her, she'd probably have clocked him.

Tried to, anyway. She was curvy and luscious—he was surprised at how well he could remember the feel of her—but she was all business, and a mama bear, to boot. She was nobody's cupcake, that was for sure.

"What are you smiling at? You got no business thinking about anything but racing when you're this close to winning the championship." The older man eyed him. "You may be a natural talent behind the wheel, but talent won't count for jack if you miss one trick out there, boy, these last three races."

Robbie was cranky—hell, everyone on the team was a bundle of nerves this close to the end, especially since all of them were aware that Andrew Clark had bet all the marbles on this championship. If they didn't win the big prize, FastMax Racing could well be forced to close its doors or, at a minimum, merge with another team or sell part interest…something that would flat kill his stepdad.

As he moved to the laptop to study the data, Garrett thought his crew chief should know him well enough to realize that nothing took his attention from racing. Women were fun, but they were fleeting. A pressure-relief valve but never a serious distraction. His mother's revolving-door marriages had convinced him that love was a pipe dream; the constant relocations had made the idea of home a foreign concept.

The closest he'd come to having a place to belong was with Andrew. He was not Andrew's blood, yet Andrew was the only man his mother had ever married who really took time to get involved with Garrett, to treat him as his own.

Which was why, once Garrett had the choice to live with whoever he wanted, he'd chosen Andrew, not his flitting butterfly mom. Andrew had first put Garrett in a quarter-midget years ago and taught him the love of racing. Andrew and Garrett's mother had divorced after only a few years, so Garrett had missed a lot of racing as a kid, but Andrew had given him a shot when he was older, and Garrett had done his best to make his stepfather proud.

Okay, not always thrilled with Garrett's behavior, no. Garrett logged more time in the NASCAR hauler than any other driver on the circuit because he tended to play things right on the edge. But Andrew simply made Garrett pay not only his own fine but the team's fine, too, and didn't harangue him.

Andrew wanted to win badly, but no worse than Garrett wanted that himself. He knew the rumors—that he was a babe magnet and popular with the fans but that he couldn't win the big one, that he'd fade in the stretch. Well, they were three races from the end, and he hadn't faded yet.

He wouldn't, either. Come hell or high water, nothing was getting between him and that championship trophy.

Not even a little blonde who looked too much like her mama.

And thought he was pretty.

Garrett smiled grimly and pointed to one line of data displayed on the screen. "There. Look at that. What are we doing about it?"

Robbie was silent for a moment, then clapped him on the back nearly hard enough to bowl him over. "All right, boy. All right. Now you're paying attention."

CHAPTER THREE

GARRETT WHEELED UP TO Grace's house, resolved to be in and out in a matter of minutes. Tomorrow he would leave for the Texas race, and he wanted to kick back a little, let off some steam before he blocked out everything to focus on the win.

He slowed a couple of houses before he reached hers and paid closer notice to the exterior, now that he'd been inside. That there was an honest-to-goodness white picket fence around the front yard made him grin. He thought those were mostly in movies, but apparently not.

The house itself was Victorian, he thought it was called that, with the curlicue stuff here and there. There were trees at the sides plus one big one in front, and different kinds of shrubs were planted right next to the house. He had no idea what kind they might be; he lived in a condo for a reason. Someday he might buy a house, but right now that seemed foolish, as much as he was on the road.

The lawn and driveway were dotted with bicycles and a scooter, three soccer balls, a football and—was that a blanket? Yep, all fluffy and pink—somehow Bella seemed the likely culprit, and Garrett wondered if her mom knew she'd taken it outside. On the porch was a wicker sofa with plump cushions, but there were signs of little girls there, too—a Barbie, a baby doll, a Ken minus clothes—plus what seemed to be a pink feather boa and more tiny dresses than half the women in town probably owned.

It was foreign territory for Garrett, but thinking about that little pistol of a girl grasping his hand and laying claim to him still made Garrett grin.

Just then, the front door and screen burst open, and not only Matthew but another boy plus a rag mop of a dog burst outside. The boys began kicking a soccer ball around while the dog chased it and barked.

Garrett parked his Carolina-blue Corvette and grabbed three packages as he emerged. The boys looked up, and Matthew's brows snapped together, instantly protective.

"Hey, guys," Garrett said easily as he used one hip to push open the front gate.

"Hey," said the other boy, his cheeks going beet-red and shuffling his feet as he glanced up at Garrett, down to the ground and back again. "Uh…how are you?"

Garrett knew the signs all too well. The boy recognized him. "I'm good. How 'bout you? Hey, Matthew."

Matthew only grunted, but his gaze returned again and again to the packages.

"I'm Garrett Clark," he said to the other boy.

"I know." The redhead's face flamed again. "I mean, yes sir, I know. You drive the No. 402 car. I eat Country Bread all the time. That's all my mama buys."

"My sponsor will be happy to hear that." Garrett shifted his packages and held out a hand to shake.

The boy awkwardly stuck out his own. "Pleased to meet you, sir."

"Same here. You got a name or shall I just make one up?"

Matthew snorted, and his friend blushed again. "No sir, I mean, yes sir, I have a name."

"It's Andy." Matthew rolled his eyes, since his friend was too busy stammering.

"Andy Calvert," said the boy.

Garrett didn't correct Matthew for being rude. He understood only too well how it felt to be a boy trying to be a man protecting his mom.

"Pleased to meet you, Andy. You two play soccer?"

"Oh, yes sir," Andy responded. "We're on the same team."

"What team is that?"

"The Tornadoes. We're sponsored by Matthew's mom."

"That right? She didn't want to name you the Chefs or something?"

Matthew snorted again, but he was grinning. "Naw, she said she thought about the Chicken Wings or maybe Potato Salad, but she was just kidding. Andy's dad said if we don't play better, he's gonna rename us the Pancakes."

Garrett burst out laughing. Andy ducked his head, but he was grinning, too. "I used to like playing soccer," Garrett said.

"Want to—would you like to maybe kick the ball around a little?" Andy asked.

Garrett glanced at Matthew for a reaction. When the boy shrugged, Garrett said, "I'm pretty rusty, but why not?" He looked around for a place to set the packages, and noticed that Matthew's eyes followed his movements. "I promised you a present."

"Yes, sir."

"Want it now or do you want to wait for your sisters?"

The conflict was written all over the boy's face, and he hesitated, but finally he shook his head. "I'll wait."

"I'm impressed. Not sure I'd have said the same at your age."

Matthew started to smile but abruptly turned away as if he couldn't allow himself that pleasure.

Garrett decided to cut the boy some slack and jogged to the other end of the open space. "Okay, let's see if I remember anything."

Garrett ran every day, so he didn't get winded at all, but the boys were quick and wily, and though he could kick a longer distance, their feet, especially Matthew's, were agile and had Garrett running twice as much. After a few minutes, however, old lessons began to emerge, and Garrett's play improved.

Andy loved playing, he could tell, but Matthew brought an

intensity to his game that would one day make him quite good. He never took his eye off the ball, and he could out-maneuver both Andy and Garrett. Garrett couldn't be sure if Matthew simply wanted to make a point or if he was always so determined, but whatever his motivation, he should be playing with much older kids.

Matthew hooked a shot that Garrett knew he'd be lucky to return when suddenly he heard a voice from the front porch.

"You came back! Look, Mommy, he came back!"

Garrett took his eyes off the ball for an instant, and it was an instant too long. Matthew threw his hands up in the air and cheered, while Andy raced over to do a chest bump.

Grace stood on the porch with her thoughts firmly hidden, but Bella leaped off the porch and came racing toward him with no heed for the older boys leaping around, feet flying.

"Bella, watch out!" Grace shouted, just as Garrett reached her and swept her up, Andy's foot barely missing her head.

Garrett's heart thudded, but the little girl only beamed. "Did you bring me a present?"

"Matthew, you and Andy have to be more careful," Grace warned. As the boys started to protest, Grace turned on Bella. "Isabella Winters, how many times have I told you to pay attention to where you're going instead of simply charging off?"

"But, Mommy, he came back." Bella smiled so sweetly that Garrett pitied the boys who'd one day cross this tiny femme fatale's path.

Her mother was apparently immune to the charm. "You are lucky that Mr. Clark has such quick reflexes, or you'd be crying your eyes out right about now, young lady." Grace looked up at him. "Thank you. She never thinks before she acts."

"My mother said the same thing often," he replied.

"Where's my present?" Bella demanded.

"Bella! Would you like to go to your room until you can find some manners?"

"But, Mommy—"

"*But Mommy* nothing. Apologize to Mr. Clark. You do not demand presents, ever."

Big blue eyes met his, two big tears trembling on thick black lashes. "I'm sorry." Then she laid her head on his shoulder, and Garrett felt himself turning into pure mush.

And maybe starting to panic a little. "Oh, don't cry, honey. It's okay, really." He looked at Grace, who was shaking her head. *Sucker,* she mouthed.

I do have a present for each of them, he said soundlessly back.

Then she, like her son before, rolled her eyes and sighed. "Would you like to come inside?" Her tone clearly indicated that it was not her first choice.

"I—let me just—"

Bella's head rose. "Come in, so I can show you my kitty, okay?" All sunshine now.

Garrett had not thought the woman existed who could manipulate him, but he was beginning to suspect he might be wrong. He glanced back at Grace. "Just for a minute, all right?"

"Yes!" Bella looked at her mother's retreating back and put her mouth to his ear, whispering, "And bring the presents."

Garrett let her shinny down to the ground and tried but could not manage to restrain his laughter. "Yes, ma'am," he responded. He went to retrieve the presents, stopping by his car to figure out something to give Andy, too.

"IT'S BRINGING COALS to Newcastle, isn't it?" Garrett murmured to Grace as Bella danced around the room with her new doll.

Grace smothered a chuckle. "To Bella, there is no such thing as having too many dolls."

"How on earth does she keep up with them?" He seemed honestly bewildered. "And why would you need more than one?"

This time Grace just let the laugh loose. "Why do you need more than one wrench? Or car?" Andy had already regaled them with a list of the vehicles Garrett owned.

"You wound me." He clapped one hand over his chest. "It's not the same thing, not at all." He pointed. "Those are toys."

"Oh, yes, and your cars would be…?"

"Important." He nodded gravely, but his eyes were twinkling. "They're not just cars, they're—"

"Man toys," Grace declared. "Big boy toys." When his eyes flew wide in mock horror, she laughed again. "I have brothers. Don't think I don't get it." But she was the one without a clue. What was she doing kidding around with this, this…*driver?* This chick magnet.

Worst of all, why was she having such a good time? "Excuse me. I have to check on something in the kitchen." And get her head on straight.

"Are you okay?"

"Fine. I'm fine." She forced herself to walk slowly and not run. Once inside, she turned and watched him with her children. Bella had gone to her room to retrieve yet another doll for him to look over, and the sheer bewilderment on his face was priceless.

Millie was retying the ribbons he'd brought for her unicorn's mane, while Matthew and Andy were in rapture over the remote-controlled car she'd had to nearly bite through her tongue to keep from refusing. Matthew had been pleading for one for two birthdays now, but she'd thought him too young.

He wasn't, she could see now. That it was a model of Garrett's own race car only made matters worse.

And somehow, he'd scrounged up a gift for Andy, too—a FastMax T-shirt several sizes too big and suspiciously not fresh out of its wrapping, but, complete with his autograph, it had thrilled Andy witless. Andy was wearing it right now, and if, as Grace suspected, it might smell of Garrett, that would only render it more valuable to her son's best friend.

She wheeled away and returned to the counter. Every single gift was unnecessary, but they'd had the effect of making her children forget all about her fainting yesterday, and the importance of that could not be discounted. Having lost their father, they tended to hover—the two older ones, at least. Bella had been too little and barely remembered Todd.

Garrett had been kissing her pastry chef in the closet only yesterday, however. She had to remember that.

"Grace?" She'd been too preoccupied to hear him approach. "You all right?" His gaze moved past her to the pot on the stove, the fresh fruit and knife on the cutting board. "Oh—sorry. I didn't think about it being suppertime. I usually eat a lot later…."

Blast it. She was going to have to invite him to dinner. Her mother would never forgive her if she didn't—fresh pain stabbed her at the thought of the mother who'd never have a chance to lecture her or hug her or listen to her ever again. A year now Linda Hunt had been gone, but Grace wasn't sure she'd ever get over missing her.

"What's wrong?"

"Nothing."

"Okay, listen, I'll just—"

"Would you like to join us?" She forced herself to face him. "I know it's early, but kids have earlier bedtimes, so I can't wait much longer to feed them."

"I—you don't have to—" He halted. "It sure smells good. And any man who'd turn down a chance to eat food like I had at that luncheon would have to be a fool."

"This isn't catered food. I cook more simply at home, at least when it's just me and the kids."

He sniffed the air. "Is that bread in the oven? Homemade bread?"

"Couldn't you smell it when you walked in the house?"

"Yeah, but I never thought—I figured it was some fancy room spray." Then he looked a little abashed. "But considering this is Gourmet by Grace's home, I guess that was pretty stupid, huh?" His expression turned wistful. "I've never had fresh homemade bread before."

To turn him away now would take a harder heart than hers. "Well, I guess you'd better stay, then."

"Can I help?"

"Do you even have a kitchen of your own?"

"Absolutely."

"And what's in the refrigerator?"

"Hmm...mustard...probably barbecue sauce in those little packets..." He shrugged. "Beer?"

"Haven't I read that you work out religiously? What on earth do you eat? Don't you think your body deserves proper fuel?"

He paused, then a slow, sexy grin spread. "You been thinking about my body, Ms. Winters?"

Her eyes went to slits. "Of course not." Just when her opinion of him was improving, he crossed the line back to the playboy she wouldn't countenance.

Even if that body was something no woman with eyes could ignore.

A yelp and a small crash sounded from the living room. She welcomed the interruption. "Since I suspect that's somehow related to your remote-controlled car, how about you go clean up the mess before I have to see it?"

He winced, but then saluted her with a cocky grin. "Yes, ma'am."

Grace watched him go, then sighed and shook her head. *Just think of him as one of the kids' friends. A really big one.*

He was certainly too much kid for her when so much else in her life was teetering.

She returned to the stove and stirred.

"ANDY, YOU TAKE THIS LOAF of bread home to your mama, okay?" Grace proffered a wrapped bundle to the boy.

Garrett had an urge to snatch it from the boy's hand. He'd had no idea something healthy could taste so incredible. He now understood why bread was associated with the term *manna from heaven.* He wasn't sure he'd ever put anything more amazing in his mouth in his whole life. Topped with real butter, Grace's whole wheat bread could make a man fall to his knees and beg.

Of course, the entire meal had been amazing. He wasn't a soup man—he preferred something he could sink his teeth into—but he quickly discovered that Grace's vegetable soup bore no resemblance to anything that came out of a can. He'd never been all that big on vegetables, either, but man…tasty and filling and, combined with her bread, all the meal a man could want. He'd had seconds and thirds and he was tight as a tick, but oh, how his stomach was dancing a happy tune.

He'd even eaten fresh fruit. She'd cut it up in shapes and somehow made it fun. She might call it a simple meal, but he'd never had a better one.

He'd been surprised, too, at how comfortable he'd felt throughout the dinner. Grace's kids were a kick, and the meal had felt so…homey, he guessed you'd call it.

The very word had always made him shudder. Strings and traps accompanied that notion of home with most of the women he'd dated. He carefully stayed away from the ones with marriage in their eyes. If he ever got married, he intended it to be for good, but with his mother's track record and the total absence of a biological father, he had no faith that he had the genes for a lasting relationship. He damn sure had no example.

A tug on his pants leg brought him to attention.

"When are you coming back?" Bella demanded, her Barbie dolls replaced by the white cat graciously allowing himself to be held like a rag doll.

Garrett rescued him and tucked one arm beneath the cat's body while scratching under his chin. "What's his name?"

"Tomi. He has pink ears. I like pink."

Garrett had to grin. "Yeah. I got that."

"Your car would be prettier if it was pink."

"He'd be laughed off the track, dork," Matthew said from the greater knowledge of an eight-year-old. He and Andy snickered.

"That's not fair." Millie looked worried about intervening. "She's not a dork."

She was so quiet and hesitant. Bella grabbed your attention and Matthew was a born leader, but Millie had already carved a special place in his heart.

"She doesn't know anything. She's just a baby," said Matthew. Bella was starting to puff up.

Garrett placed a hand on Millie's shoulder in camaraderie. "Guess you didn't notice when I drove a pink car for the pink ribbon campaign, huh?" he asked the boys. "I even had pink on my uniform."

Bella was radiant. Millie glanced up at him for confirmation, and he winked at her. "It's true." He glanced at Andy and Matthew. "Wearing pink doesn't make a man less of a man, you know." Though he had to admit that a pink car was not his ideal, either, but he wouldn't tell them that.

"Well, I better go." Obviously unconvinced of Garrett's last point, Andy made for the front door. "Goodbye, sir. And thank you for the shirt."

"You're welcome. If you ever get to a race, let me know and I'll show you around."

"For real?" Andy's eyes were huge. "Oh, man. Wait'll I tell my dad!" He grasped the knob as though ready to charge home, then stopped. "Um, thanks for dinner, Mrs. Winters. See you at the bus tomorrow," he said to Matthew.

Then he was gone. Garrett knew his own departure needed to be soon, but he found himself curiously reluctant to leave. "Well, guess I should head out, too."

"Don't go," pleaded Bella.

"Bella, it's bath time, and Mr. Clark has to leave town in the morning for Texas, I think," Grace admonished.

"Will you come back?" she repeated.

"I don't know, honey…" He set the cat down in preparation and cast a glance at Grace, whose features betrayed nothing. Certainly no enthusiasm.

"Millie, go help Bella pick out her pajamas," Grace said firmly. "Matthew, you get your backpack ready for tomorrow."

Millie leaned against his leg for an instant so brief he might have imagined it. "Bye, Mr. Clark." She clasped her little sister's hand. "Thank you for the ribbons."

"You'll come back," Bella ordered. At a look from her mother, she spoke again. "Thank you for the doll." Then she allowed herself to be led away.

"Thank you for the car. It's awesome," Matthew said.

"You're very welcome."

"Good luck at Texas. I was a Kent Grosso fan, but I want you to win the championship now."

Garrett grinned, despite the nerves that kicked up at Matthew's statement. "Thanks." Odd how one boy's wish could unsettle him as no other pressure had done.

"I'll be right there," Grace called to her children, then reached for the door handle, obviously more than ready to see him go. "Thank you for helping me clean up," she said with the same excellent manners she'd taught her children.

"I still owe some on my debt. That was the best meal I ever had in my life."

She seemed surprised. "I like feeding people."

"Guess so. You're sure good at it."

An awkward silence descended.

"Well…" He stirred himself and shrugged on his jacket. "Thank you again." He leaned in to bestow a friendly kiss on her cheek.

Startled, Grace turned her head abruptly, and his mouth grazed hers.

They both froze. Garrett couldn't recall ever feeling so awkward, yet those soft, lush lips sang a siren song, and he couldn't move away. "Can I come back, Grace?"

She went rigid. Her pupils were big and dark and her eyes studied his, oddly naked. For a second, he had the strangest feeling of…connection.

Grace stepped back. "I have children."

He straightened. "I know that."

"They come first."

"I did fine with them, didn't I?" He had no idea why he was pushing. She was so not his type. The food had gone to his head or something—maybe there was some weird ingredient in it that could account for how atypically he was behaving.

"It's easy to be Santa Claus." She turned away from him and reached for a bundle on the entry table. "Here—let this be part of a more nutritious breakfast than I'm guessing you normally eat."

"Is this—?" He sniffed and could tell it was another loaf of her bread. "Oh, man. I can't let any of the guys find out about this. Or maybe I should share, and the whole team will bond." He abandoned the argument he'd been about to have with her, relieved to put things back on safe ground. "You may have just provided the magic ingredient for a win at Texas." He grimaced. "I need it. The points are so tight that a win has never been more important."

"Good luck, Garrett." She held out a hand for a business-like shake.

People had always said he was like a dog with a bone when he wanted something, that he was perversely stubborn. He didn't want Grace, not the way she'd insist, not the forever way. He wasn't made of that, even if he wanted to be.

He didn't. But for whatever reason, he wasn't through with her, either. So instead of shaking, he lifted her hand and pressed his lips to it. Not the palm as he might have with someone else—he had a sense he was just shy of getting slapped down—but on the back of it.

Still, she looked a bit stunned by the gesture and waited a little too long to retrieve her hand from his grasp.

Then she straightened. Took a step back. "Goodbye, Garrett."

Though he wasn't as sanguine about her presence as he wanted her to believe, damned if she didn't still bring the devil out in him, so he grinned and raised one eyebrow. And refused to say goodbye.

"Good night, Grace. Sweet dreams."

The door closed very decisively behind him.

CHAPTER FOUR

"SON, I DON'T HAVE TO TELL you that with three races left and you, Justin Murphy and Will Branch within less than fifty points of each other, a win would be very welcome right now." Andrew Clark kept his tone light.

But Garrett understood that the situation was deadly serious. "Just as long as I play it safe at the same time, right, Dad?" The stakes were both personal and professional for his stepfather. Garrett was in second place to Justin, who had married into the Grosso clan, though he didn't drive for their team. Patsy Grosso was Andrew's sister, and Andrew was sick of playing a distant second fiddle to the golden Grossos, NASCAR royalty.

Will Branch was behind Garrett and no one to take lightly. Having a wife and newfound son had settled Will down from his wild bachelor days, and with Zoe expecting twins, Will had a lot of mouths to feed.

Garrett didn't want Will's kids to go hungry, but they wouldn't even if Will didn't win the championship, while there were people working at FastMax who might lose their jobs if Garrett didn't pull off this title run.

"Just don't go off half-cocked," Andrew said. He clapped Garrett on the shoulder. "I trust you. You know that."

Yeah. That was the killer part. Everyone at FastMax had busted their buns to make this championship happen. They'd keep doing their best to see that he had what he needed—fast pit stops, powerful equipment under him, sharp minds focused on only one thing: winning.

But in the end, it was up to him.

For a fleeting second, he wished he could drop in on Grace's haven, just sit down and breathe in a little of the peace he'd found amidst the lively, kid-induced chaos of her home.

He'd toasted some of her bread this morning for good luck.

And his mind kept returning to that kiss—ridiculous, since it could barely be called one, it had been so brief.

"Garrett? Did you hear what I said?" His stepfather's voice yanked him out of his musings.

She's not for you, boy, he reminded himself. *She's a nice lady, but she's got Serious Candidates Only written all over her.*

Though in truth, she'd never shown a sign she was interested…and he shouldn't be. *Wasn't.*

"Garrett?" He was saved from answering Andrew by the sound of his aunt's voice.

"Hey, Aunt Patsy." Though Patsy Grosso wasn't blood kin, he'd known her for much of his life and been treated like one of the family.

"I know you and Justin have to be mortal enemies out there on the track today, but I just wanted to come wish you and Andrew a good race."

"Thanks." He bent to kiss her cheek and let her hug him. She seemed fragile these days. Having spent the entire season with a mystery blogger trumpeting to the world that the daughter she'd thought kidnapped and dead as an infant might still be alive was wearing on her and Dean both—the whole family, really. "You okay?"

She cupped his cheek. "I'm fine." The shadows beneath her eyes said differently.

"Man, I wish— Sorry. It doesn't help you to bring up the rumors, does it? Whoever that idiot blogger is should be horsewhipped for causing you so much pain."

She seemed startled. "Haven't you heard? The blogger has been identified. It's Susan Winters."

He frowned, not recognizing the name until… His eyes went wide. "*Winters?* Any kin to Grace?"

"You know Grace?"

Well, at least news of him being caught in the closet before the luncheon hadn't made the rounds, though he had no idea how he'd escaped. NASCAR was a small, intimate family, and word usually got out quickly. "Uh, yeah, I mean, everybody knows about her, with the TV show and the catering…"

"Susan is her former mother-in-law, and Susan's son Tony Winters—"

"—is the guy who confessed to killing Alan Cargill," he finished for her. He still couldn't get over that. Imagine how Grace must feel.

"Right," Patsy said, "Tony was Grace's partner after her husband died, in charge of the company's finances, and he had been skimming money from the operation." Patsy shook her head. "Her children are his blood, but he has the gall to steal food from their mouths? If Grace didn't already work harder than any five people I know, she'd probably have gone under already. Then to lose her mother just a year ago after being widowed the year before…that girl is made of strong stuff."

Not so strong that she can't break, he thought. He felt worse than ever about adding to her strain. "Man…that's rough." And she'd invited him to her home—cooked for him, even. When she probably needed to just go to bed for a month.

"Oops, time for driver introductions. Better get back to the war wagon," she said. "Good luck, Garrett. And safe racing." She pressed a kiss to his cheek and was gone.

"You all right?" asked Andrew.

"Me? Yeah, sure. Always." He pasted on a smile. "It's gonna be fine today, Dad. The car's good, and I love this track. I'll do you proud, I promise."

"You always do, son." Andrew gave him a back-thumping man hug and waved him off.

Garrett did his best to wipe Grace Winters out of his mind. He would, though, stop in and check on her when he returned to North Carolina.

But there was no room for anything but racing now.

THE DOORBELL RANG THAT NIGHT after she'd gotten the kids to bed, and Grace wondered who would be at her house at this hour.

For a traitorous second, she wondered if it might be Garrett, and she was instantly chagrined by the notion. Even if he hadn't had a near disaster on the track this afternoon, he wouldn't be back in Charlotte yet.

Not that she wanted him to visit.

When she peered through the glass in her front door, she was more than shocked to see her father, Ethan and Hope on the other side.

A shudder went through her. They never used the front door or rang the bell. Someone was hurt or—

She couldn't think about another loss. She yanked open the door. "Is Jared okay? Ethan, are Sadie and Cassie all right?"

"Cassie's with Sadie, and they're okay," Ethan answered. "Jared's fine, too. He's burning the midnight oil at FastMax."

"Is—did something happen to Garrett?" Jared was the engine builder for Garrett's cars—but no, he'd finished the race, though he'd had a close call.

"Garrett? Garrett Clark, you mean?" Ethan's confusion laid that concern to rest immediately. "Why would you ask that?"

Hope was looking at her oddly. "After how he behaved at the luncheon the other day, why would you care? I thought you were furious with him."

Uh-oh. Grace cursed herself for blurting that out and tried to dodge. "He's apologized profusely. And you saw how he even brought the kids presents to make up to Millie, especially, for scaring her." She seized the moment. "So why exactly are you all here, with such long faces?"

They exchanged glances. She felt a little on the outside

looking in, an experience she hadn't had in this family since she was three.

"Let's sit down, sweetheart," urged Dan Hunt, not her birth father but the man who'd raised her and certainly the father of her heart.

"What is it, Daddy? Are you—is something wrong? Are you sick?"

He shook his head. "I'm mad as hell, but my health is fine."

"So what is everyone doing here?" A hard knot inside her eased a bit at the realization that everyone she loved was safe, but she could tell that something was definitely wrong.

"Come sit with me," said Ethan, the big brother who'd always been special to the little girl he'd welcomed so long ago. He'd been her protector, her guide, her rock.

"You're scaring me. Just spit it out, someone. What's going on?"

He exhaled in a gust. "The news will be all over town soon. We didn't want you to hear from somewhere else."

Finally Dan spoke again. "There's no good way to break this. It's about Linda."

"Mom? But—" *She's dead,* Grace wanted to protest, but her stepbrothers were every bit as devastated by the loss as she was, even if only she and Hope had Linda as a birth mother.

"Susan Winters says that Mom participated in kidnapping the Grosso baby."

It was like someone had dropped a bomb in the middle of the room. "What?" Grace looked at each of them. "That's outrageous! Mom would never—"

Ethan slipped his arm around her shoulder from one side, and her dad took her hand from the other. "We don't believe it, either, but she claims that Mom confessed to this right before she died, and Susan tried to alert the police with an anonymous tip they ignored. She sent Dean and Patsy a letter but never heard from them. Mom never told her any details, though, so Susan has no idea where the baby ended up. She started blogging because she didn't know how else to give Patsy and Dean a chance to know that Kent's twin didn't die as they'd been told. She told all this to Evie, who has taken it to Jake McMasters."

"I—" Grace was surprised to feel more puzzled than anything else, right this minute. Pain lurked, she knew, if this ever seemed real, but at the moment, it was simply preposterous. "How—let alone why—would Mom ever be in a position to kidnap a baby?"

"That's the thing," Dan said. "Susan says Linda was once a nurse. That she worked in the Nashville hospital where Gina Grosso was born and disappeared."

"Nashville? When was that?"

"The same year you were born," Hope said. "Only a few months after."

"Mom always said she never worked outside the home. She didn't believe day care was good for a child. After my father died, she lived off his insurance money until we moved here and she married Dad. She wouldn't lie." Grace turned to her father. "She wasn't a nurse." But her tone was more question than certainty.

"Not that I ever knew," Dan replied. "I mean, she was good at patching up you four, but any mother learns to do that."

Grace recalled something Ethan had said earlier. "Who's Jake McMasters?"

"He's Patsy Grosso's cousin. A private investigator they hired to help them figure out who Gina Grosso is now. He's been helping them weed through the pretenders who keep popping up."

"I want to talk to him," she said.

"I've already given him a piece of my mind, sis. He's actually not a bad guy. We could be in worse hands."

"But we're supposed to just sit here and let our mother be dragged through the dirt? Let Daddy have people looking at him, at all of us, with pity or worse?"

"I'm thinking of finding our own detective to clear Mom of this insane accusation," Ethan declared.

They all considered that idea in silence.

Then Hope spoke up. "Grace? I know you were small when Mom and Daddy married, but is there anything at all you might remember if you thought hard?"

Grace wrinkled her forehead. "I don't have any real memory of when we didn't live here. I remember the first time I saw Ethan, at least I think it was the first time." She turned to him. "You seemed ten feet tall. Jared was occupied demonstrating that he was too cool to consort with a mere girl, but you…" She leaned against Ethan's shoulder and clasped his arm. "You crouched down and said 'hi' to me. Even admired my doll."

Ethan tipped his head to hers. "You were like a doll yourself, all big blue eyes and blond curls. A lot like Bella is now—if Bella had a shy bone in her body, that is."

Everyone chuckled.

Grace returned to Hope's question. "I'll think hard about it, but three is so young. I don't know that I'll come up with anything."

Dan shifted and placed his chin in his hands, a favorite position for reflection. "I'll talk to Jake. Linda was the best wife a man could want and one incredible mother, even to two wild, half-grown boys. She would never have harmed a child, I'd stake my life on it."

"Amen," said Ethan. "I don't know what Susan's problem is, but she's either lying or severely mistaken. Whatever, she owes Mom an apology." He rose. "Don't you worry about this, sis. I should have known you wouldn't crumple like some fragile flower." Then his set features thawed a little. "Oops. You did that already, didn't you?"

Grace rose and mock-punched him in the gut. He did a boxing shuffle. "Don't hurt me, killer. Anyway, tell me more about Garrett."

"There's nothing to tell, except that Bella wants to keep him because he's pretty."

Ethan laughed. "Well, after that stunt he pulled today trying to win the race and nearly wrecking, Andrew may give him to her free of charge."

"He made it back to finish fourth," Hope pointed out.

"Yes, but Will won the race and pulled closer in points, and Justin finished one spot ahead and held their margin. He's got two races left to get in front of Justin in points, and absolutely no margin for error," Ethan responded.

"Boy's got guts galore behind the wheel," Dan said. "But he's a crew chief's nightmare, never knowing what maverick move he'll pull next."

"He'll be lucky if there's any hide left on him after Andrew gets through with him. That team is strapped for sponsorship money, and Andrew has gambled everything on Garrett winning. There could be no FastMax at Daytona next season if Garrett doesn't win this championship."

"Is he just reckless, or stupid and careless to boot?" Grace wondered.

"Reckless," Ethan opined. "Jared says he's hell on his engines."

"Boy's not stupid," Dan said. "He's clawed his way to the top tier of drivers, mainly through a lot of daring moves, usually at the right time. It's only that when he's wrong, it can cost him. Dollars to doughnuts Andrew told him to play things safe today."

"But if he had pulled off that pass, he'd have won going away," Ethan noted.

In the ensuing silence, Hope spoke. "Sounds like he's carrying a lot of expectations on his shoulders."

"From what I've heard, being around all these years," Dan offered, "more expectations than you realize. His mother actually dumped him with Andrew. Andrew's his stepfather, not his birth dad."

"Wow," responded Ethan.

Wow, indeed, Grace thought. The playboy might be more complex than she'd guessed. Then she inadvertently yawned. "Sorry—long day."

"We'll get out of your hair," Ethan said. "But first—are you okay? I mean, as okay as any of us can be about all this?"

"I'm not going to fall apart, if that's what you mean. But I'm not happy, and I want answers."

Dan nodded. "I'll call Jake first thing in the morning and see what he has, then we'll talk about whether we want to hire our own man." He drew Grace close and pressed a kiss to her forehead. "You go to bed, little girl. You look tuckered out."

She leaned against the man who'd always been a tower of strength for her. "I am, Daddy, I have to admit."

"You've had a lot thrown at you the last couple of years, and after what Tony did to you…"

"I'd just like one shot at him," Ethan fumed. "Hope he rots in jail." He looked at Grace. "Uh, you okay for money, sis? That bastard robbed you blind, didn't he?"

"Not blind," she reassured her protective family. "We won't starve. I won't say it didn't hurt—the kids' college funds won't get any additions soon without me firing staff, and that's something I don't want to do—can't afford to, really. We get more business every day. I have to float expenses ahead, so it's tight, I won't kid you." She hugged her father again. "But the kids and I will be fine. Especially with the cookbook coming out in three months and who knows what evolving from that?"

"So our sister the TV star can still buy herself some snazzy stilettos?" Hope asked.

Grace rolled her eyes. "Even if I liked crippling myself, being on my feet all day is punishment enough, thank you. I'll leave you to be the Stiletto Queen."

"Brent does like the way they make my legs look," Hope responded.

"TMI, little sis. I don't even want to think about you having sex," said Ethan with a shudder.

"And on that note, I believe I'll usher this group of ruffians outside," Dan said. "'Night, sweetheart. I'll call you tomorrow, and I'll pick the kids up after school, as usual."

"I don't know what I'd do without you, Daddy. You're my hero."

Dan's cheeks stained with color. "And you're my angel, punkin." He grasped Hope around the shoulders. "One angel and one princess," he declared, then looked at his son with a grin. "Okay, and two demons. Oh, well. A man needs some balance in his life."

Grace watched her family go, warmed as always by the love she'd been surrounded by since the lucky day her mother met Dan Hunt.

Her mother. A kidnapper? It couldn't be true. Absolutely could not.

GARRETT KNEW HE WAS WASTING a trip. It was after midnight, and there was school tomorrow. Grace would be asleep.

But his conversation with Patsy wouldn't let go of him—and he was too disgusted with himself to sleep, anyway. If he went back to that condo he barely inhabited, he'd just be flipping through TV channels as he attempted to settle the dread crowding his chest.

He'd blown it. Yeah, he'd finished fourth, but Justin had come in third, collecting five more points than him and a bonus five points for leading at least one lap. Garrett had collected five himself for leading a lap, but still, the margin between them had increased by five.

Worse, Will Branch had won the race, thereby narrowing the gap between himself and Garrett to only seventeen.

With two races left and how much of racing was sheer luck, any of them could win the championship. Not winning wouldn't be the ruin of Justin or Will, but FastMax had a sponsor who was looking toward Will, now that he was a family man, as perhaps the type of driver they needed. Families with children bought a lot of loaves of bread, and Will's twin babies plus that photogenic Sam had the marketing people drooling.

It didn't matter how much Garrett could argue that he absolutely wouldn't have finished in the top ten had he not gone for the pass. The fact was that he had been in third at that point with enough laps left to possibly take the lead. Rafael O'Bryan's car had gotten loose and nearly taken out both of them. It had taken every skill Garrett had to escape the wall with only a scrape.

But he had. Fact was, he'd fallen back to eleventh and had to fight with everything in him to reach the front before the race ended. Fourth was a moral victory, yes, but he had promised his dad he'd be patient, and he hadn't been.

At the corner where he should turn toward Grace's cul-de-sac, Garrett nearly went straight. He sat at the stop sign for a long time, barely able to see her house.

They were nothing to each other.

They were as opposite as two people could be.

But—

That *but* was the problem. He couldn't put a finger on why Grace appealed to him, why he couldn't seem to forget her. A week ago, he'd only known her by name.

But for whatever reason, he wished he could just be with her in that house that was so different from anything in his experience. Take a good look at her, after what he'd learned today about her troubles, and see if she needed a friend, too. That was all they could be, but something about being with Grace settled him.

Which should disturb the hell out of him. Settling was so not his style.

A flicker of light caught his attention, and he thought it might be coming from her house. He made the turn, after all, only to be sure everything was all right. As he approached, he realized that the light was indeed emanating from her house, in the vicinity of the kitchen, splashing onto the bushes outside the old farmhouse table where her family ate meals.

He parked and walked closer, just to be certain. A burglar was hardly likely to turn on the lights, but still…

Through the window, he spotted her, those lush curves wrapped in a soft blue robe the color of her eyes, her head bent to her hands.

She was crying.

Normally, Garrett did anything possible to avoid a woman in tears. What man ever knew how to deal with them? There was no good reason for tears—ever. Not in his book. Crying had to mean disaster, regardless of the women who'd tried to convince him that happy tears existed.

Grace's posture telegraphed clearly that these were not tears of joy.

Before he could think it through, he circled around to the side door beneath the carport and knocked on the window. "Grace, it's me, Garrett." He identified himself immediately so as not to frighten her.

She rose, and he watched her avert her face, swipe at her cheeks and reach for a tissue, seeking to erase what she'd been doing. She approached the door hesitantly. "What are you doing here?" she asked through the glass.

"Let me in. Please."

"It's late, Garrett."

"I know." He was almost positive that if he gave her a choice, she'd send him away, but she looked as though she could use a friend, too, so he held firm.

She unlocked the door but only held it open a few inches. "What is it?" She was trying to look annoyed and probably was, but she also looked vulnerable, her face scrubbed clean of any makeup, her hair in disarray, her eyes sorrowful. She grasped the neck of her robe and closed it over the expanse of smooth pale skin he couldn't help noticing.

"May I come in?"

"Why?"

Man, she didn't give in easily. He had the inescapable sense that if he referred to her tears before he managed to get inside, she'd never let him in. He had no choice but to appeal to the nurturer in her. "I had a crappy race." He allowed her to see the truth of his misery.

Her face relaxed a little. "You finished fourth."

"Barely. I gambled again when I promised I wouldn't."

She smiled softly and stepped back to let him inside. "Do you do that a lot?"

"Break promises?" He shook his head. "No, but I…" He shrugged. "I take chances. Mostly they pay off."

"But not today."

"Not today. There's so much at stake. FastMax is in trouble. I have to win this championship."

"Would you like some tea?" She was already bustling at the stove, filling a teapot and getting mugs from the cabinet.

He barely resisted a grimace. "I guess."

"Not a manly enough drink for a big, bad driver?"

He was forced to smile. "Something like that. Don't you have to know how to crook your little finger or something?"

She chuckled. "Such a guy. How about hot chocolate, then?"

"Do I get marshmallows? The big ones?"

"Sure, tough guy. The little ones not manly, either?" She turned off the kettle and retrieved milk and cream from the refrigerator and began heating the milk. Then she opened a cabinet, took out a bar of chocolate, and began shaving it.

"Where's the little packets?"

Her look was pure pity. "I said hot chocolate, not chocolate water."

"Wow. I've never had the real thing. Man, how do you know all this stuff? I mean, you're like Betty Crocker or June Cleaver or something."

She waved the utensil at him in a vaguely threatening

manner. "Insults will only get you thrown out of my kitchen, pronto." She resumed shaving, the pile of chocolate growing.

"Sorry." He held out his hands in surrender. "But I meant no insult. I think it's amazing. Truly, how did you learn to do all this? I mean, it's like you actually, well, like it."

She laughed. "And that's a shock?"

"Well, hey, I mean, we all need to eat and stuff, but you're going to all this trouble, and it's not even for a job."

Another shake of the head. "I'll say it again. You are such a guy."

"Is that so bad?"

Her gaze met his, and the moment pulsated with their awareness of each other. Between the smell of chocolate plus some even better scent that seemed to emanate from her skin, and watching those unpainted lips as she talked…

She looked away first, ducking her head to concentrate. "No," she said quietly. "Men are a pretty wonderful species, I've always thought."

Not a come-on at all, simple fact, he thought, but the effect on him was like gas on a fire.

Grace Winters was the real deal—all woman, every inch of her. No boy hips, no fake tan, none of the hard glamour of the females who comprised so much of his experience.

Down, boy. Unlike his usual response to a turn-on, he scrambled to escape a moment neither of them were ready for.

"So…did your mother like to cook?"

She nodded but kept her head down. "She—she taught me—" Abruptly, Grace dropped the chocolate and the utensil and whirled away.

"Grace? What is it?" He rounded the bar he'd been keeping safely between them and turned her toward him, though she resisted.

He caught her chin. "Hey, I'm sorry. I know that she died. I didn't mean to—"

Grace shook off his apology, but tears kept coming.

He was so not good with tears, but he was all she had. Awkwardly he gathered her into his arms.

For a moment she froze, but when he held on, she crumpled against him and sobbed.

And for a span, he wasn't even as aware of how amazing her body felt against him as he was conscious of how it seemed oddly right for her to be there, in his arms. *Sweet Mother MacCree, this can't be,* he thought. Even if she were his type, the timing could not be worse.

Yet still he held her, and rocked her gently.

Suddenly, she stiffened with alarm. "The milk!"

He reached around her and lifted the pan from the burner, setting it aside. "Forget the chocolate. Talk to me."

"I can't. I don't want to." She busied herself scrubbing at the counter, but then her shoulders sagged. "I miss her, yes," she whispered. "Terribly. But that's not why I can't sleep."

"Tell me."

The story spilled out then, the accusation that her mother had kidnapped Patsy and Dean's baby girl.

"Man." That rocked him back on his heels. "Aunt Patsy told me about Susan Winters being the blogger, but…wow."

"Aunt Patsy." She retreated a step. "I forgot—you're related. This is even worse."

"We're not actually related. Patsy is Andrew's sister, yes, but Andrew's my stepdad, not my father."

"Doesn't matter. You're family. You must hate me. She surely will." Grace pressed her lips together. "Even though it's not true. It can't be true, but I have no idea how to prove it. And I can't imagine why Susan is lying about this. She's my children's grandmother, for heaven's sake."

"Even if your mother did it, you're not responsible, Grace."

"She didn't." Her tone brooked no argument. "She would never do something like that. Anyway, why would she? I was already there, only a few months old. She didn't need a baby herself, and the mother I knew would never have stolen a child then, what, given it away? Sold it? Nothing about this makes sense. For that matter, how do we even know that Gina Grosso is still alive? It's only Susan's word, and Susan has been more than a little messed-up for quite a while." Her chin jutted. "She was my mother's best friend—or so my mother thought. We were in and out of her house my entire childhood. I married her son, gave her grandbabies. I thought she loved me." Grace's hands fisted, and she began to pace. "This will be all over NASCAR by morning. It's killing my father and my brothers and Hope, and it's just not true. It can't be—but how do I prove it?"

"Why not go to the police?"

"It happened in Nashville. The authorities here don't have a stake."

"A private investigator?"

"Evie already went to one, Jake McMasters. Apparently he's been working for Patsy and Dean ever since the first rumors broke, trying to track down Gina. Besides, he's Patsy's cousin." Grace sighed. "I've always been fond of the Grossos. I've catered events for them, and I like their whole family. My heart aches for them, and I absolutely want them to find their baby if she's alive, but…"

"Patsy likes you, too. She told me she admires how hard you work and what a success you're making of yourself. She's a wonderful person, and she'd be the first to tell you this is not on your shoulders, even if it is true."

"And what am I supposed to tell my children when they hear the rumors? How are they supposed to feel when they hear their beloved Nana's name being dragged in the dirt?" She threw out her hands. "It's not true, Garrett. My mother was never a nurse, and she would have cut off her arm rather than harm a child. She adored children, and she loved her family. We cannot let her be slandered."

"Patsy would meet with you, I'm sure."

"No! The last thing I want to do is to face them." Her head

dropped into her hands. "I'm taping a show at the Phoenix race, and I've already committed to a sponsor event," she groaned. "How do I deal with everyone in NASCAR, knowing that they're all thinking horrible things about my mother behind my back?"

"You hold your head up straight and tell them what you told me. They can take a flying leap if they don't believe you."

"Easy for you to say." She looked so young, so small and fragile.

"Invite me to your event, whatever it is. And you can spend time with me and my team when you're not working," he said impulsively. Just as quickly, he wondered what on earth he was doing.

She looked every bit as startled. "One event is on Saturday while you'll be practicing. The other is in your sponsor's suite during the race. You'll be a little busy."

"Oh." He thought for a minute, wondered about having a word with the CEO of Country Bread, but he knew that he had to be very careful with an already shaky sponsor. "Well, the offer to hang out stands." Even though he was already regretting it. He did not need the distraction Grace presented.

"Thanks, but you can't shield me from this, if that's what you're trying to do." Her eyes softened. "Are you always so chivalrous, Garrett Clark?"

"You know I'm not." He readied himself to leave. "Listen, I'll talk to Patsy for you, if you'd like."

"Don't you have enough worries of your own?" She stood straight and became, once again, the woman who was younger than him, he was almost certain, but managed three children while carving out an impressive career for herself. "Look, Garrett, both of us have a lot on our plates. I appreciate the shoulder—" though she looked more chagrined than grateful for it "—but the episode at the luncheon is behind us, and you don't owe me or my children any more apologies. We'll be all right, and meanwhile, you have two tough races ahead of you. I'm sure you'd rather not be bothered with my family issues." Suddenly, she was all but booting him out the door as she ushered him across the kitchen floor.

Then she granted him a smile that was gracious and polite but held nothing of the woman he'd glimpsed as she wept in his arms. "We'll all be rooting for you at Phoenix and Homestead."

Garrett tried to remember the last time a woman had brushed him off.

He couldn't. He was so astonished at the oddity of it that he was outside before he knew what had hit him. He had no idea what sort of goodbye he'd mumbled, but one thing was inescapably clear:

Grace Winters didn't want him in her life.

Which should be an enormous relief, because he didn't need her in his, either.

He walked to his car, got in and drove home. Unlocked the door, threw his keys on the bar and removed his shirt on his way to bed.

But as he lay in the darkness trying to relax enough to sleep, a burr of discontent lingered, and figuring out the nature of it took a long time, though finally he got it.

Racing was all he knew and all that mattered. He *should* be relieved that he was free of Grace, that he'd escaped her turmoil and was solidly back into the life he knew best.

But somehow, blast it, he was not.

CHAPTER FIVE

"You positive you don't want to stay in my motor home, Grace?" Ethan asked as they deplaned in Phoenix. He took his role as her big brother very seriously.

"Thank you, but no. Cassie and Sadie will be here tomorrow, and I'd need to move anyway. My room at the hotel is all set."

"You sure you're all right after hearing about Dad's conversation with Jake?"

"Are any of us?" she asked. "I mean, he says Jake seems like a good guy, but now Jake's got that New York detective Haines from the Cargill case involved again. I still don't understand why."

"Jared asked about that. Seems that Mattie Clayton insisted to Haines from early on that she had an instinct that there was a connection between the Cargill murder and the Grosso baby kidnapping, though she couldn't prove it."

Grace shivered at the mention of Mattie. They'd gone to high school together, though they hadn't been friends. Mattie was a reporter now and had been covering Alan Cargill's murder when she'd tried to keep Tony from fleeing the country before being arrested. Grace had been with Tony at the time, unaware of any of it. He'd held both of them at gunpoint, trying to silence Mattie and make his escape.

"Why would there be any connection between the two?"

"Beats me, but Jake remembered Haines talking about that, so he called him to see if Haines could shed any light on it. Haines isn't involved legally, I don't think, he's just curious."

"Seems to be going around. I don't look forward to this weekend. I've had enough pitying looks in Charlotte to last me a lifetime."

"I hear you." His jaw tightened. "Which is why you should stay with us."

She found a smile then and pressed one hand to his cheek. "Did anyone ever tell you, Ethan Hunt, that you are a very good man? What would I have done without you in my life?"

His eyes were warm on hers. "Probably had fewer boyfriends disappear after the first-date treatment Jared and I gave them. Todd's the only one who stuck."

"He had an advantage. He knew you when you weren't so big and tough."

Ethan's fond expression sobered as they both thought about all the years the Hunt and Winters kids had grown up practically in each other's pockets.

Then a shout from his teammates caught Ethan's attention. "Looks like the car's going to leave without us. We'll drop you off at the hotel first before we go to the track, if you're determined to stay there."

"I am." She threw her arms around him and hugged him hard. "But I adore you, big brother." She lingered in the arms that had sheltered her for as long as she could remember.

Then she stepped back, grabbed her bag and readied herself for a weekend she couldn't help dreading.

GARRETT TOOK THE STAIRS two at a time, reluctant to wait for the elevator going up to the sponsor suites. He'd drawn a qualifying slot way down the order, and he was late to the sponsor event. When Andrew had asked him to make a special effort to attend, he hadn't notified Grace. No point, after the bum's rush she'd given him the other night.

He was pretty happy with his qualifying run, even if he'd missed the pole by a tenth of a second. He'd start up front, and he intended to stay there.

As he loped down the hall toward the suite, one of the girls who worked for track management broke into a delighted smile as she stood guard outside. "Mr. Clark. Right in here." She gestured and turned the knob. "And congratulations on qualifying second."

"Thanks." He took a deep breath, smoothed down his sweaty hair and steeled himself.

"The food's amazing," she murmured. "Be sure and get some."

"You bet." The mention of Grace's cooking didn't serve to steady him—he not only had to charm the sponsor's people but deal with his own inexplicable reactions to Grace.

He stepped inside. Andrew was nearby and gestured him over. The silver-haired man with him turned. "Well, there's our boy. Great qualifying run, son. How's the car?" asked Mel Springer, CEO of Country Bread.

"She's a sweet one, sir. Got a good feeling about her." Even if that had been a lie, he knew this was the time to keep things positive. However tempting, he didn't believe in making excuses for himself. "We're ready to race."

"Good, good," his sponsor replied. "What would you like to drink? How about a beer?"

"No, thank you. After tomorrow's race, sure, but not until then."

Springer and Andrew exchanged looks. "I like this boy. Keeps his eye on the prize."

Andrew nodded. "Garrett's got a good head on his shoulders."

"Except sometimes he gets a little aggressive, right?"

"Being passive doesn't win races," Garrett replied. But however the insinuation stung, he owed them a sop. "There's a fine line between caution and cowardice that's not always easy to see when you're in the middle of the moment. I intend to be careful tomorrow, but I can't shy back from giving it my all." Garrett could almost feel Andrew's tension.

The sponsor was quiet for a second, then clapped Garrett

on the shoulder. "That's what we count on you for, son. You always do give it your all, and the fans love that. But we'd sure like to take that championship back to headquarters next week."

No pressure, of course, Garrett thought. But if you couldn't take the heat, you didn't belong in the car. "I intend to see that you do, sir."

"That's my boy. Come on, there's some folks I'd like you to meet. And—" Springer bent closer "—better get some of this incredible food before the troops leave only crumbs. I tell you, that Grace Winters is really something. Worth every penny we paid to fly her and her supplies and assistant in. You ever eaten any of her cooking?"

Garrett couldn't help but flash back to a cold night, a cozy dinner, a house filled with warmth. "Yes, sir, I sure have."

"Then you know." The sponsor turned away.

Andrew held him back for a second. "You did a great job down there, Garrett."

"Wish I'd gotten us the pole."

"Doesn't matter. You got us on the front row, and I'm betting you'll keep us there all day."

Garrett felt his gut tighten a little more, but he only smiled and nodded, then turned to follow the CEO.

Several introductions later, after thoroughly analyzing the track condition, the weather forecast and the rest of the field, Garrett at last had a chance to make his way over to the food.

But all he saw was Grace. She looked good enough to eat herself. He wondered if a red apron with checkered flag borders had ever looked so hot on anyone else.

Not that she didn't appear completely professional and competent, with her blond hair upswept, her white shirt and black pants as spotless and well-creased as though she'd only now donned them. Cool, calm and totally in control.

It made him want to mess her up.

"Hello, Garrett. Congratulations on your run," she said as if they were only polite acquaintances.

"Thanks. Everyone's raving about your food." He popped a meatball in his mouth and nearly moaned. "Oh, man, that's awesome. I am starving. I can't ever eat before qualifying." He scoured the table, trying to decide what to grab next. A lot of it.

Just then, a brunette in a tight dress and killer heels sidled up. "Garrett," she cooed. "Hi, I'm Josie. I just thought I'd die when you and Rafael nearly wrecked at Texas. I was so worried about you." Slick red lips glistened as she wetted the lower one with her tongue. "Come sit with me and my friends and tell us all about it, won't you?"

"Uh—" He cast a quick glance at Grace, who only lifted her eyebrows. He apologized with his eyes, hoping she understood that he had to make nice here.

"I'll bring you a plate, Mr. Clark," Grace said in a saccharine tone that made him wince. "Is there anything you don't like or can't eat?"

"Um, Josie, how about if I join you in a second? Where are you sitting?"

"We're over there, but I can wait. I don't mind a bit, Garrett," she assured him in a breathy voice.

"Well, see, I have to talk to Grace here about my appearance on her TV show."

A flicker of interest had the blonde noticing Grace as more than the woodwork this time. "You have a TV show?"

"This is Grace Winters of Gourmet by Grace. A national network has picked up her show, and she's bringing out a NASCAR cookbook at Daytona next year."

"I don't cook," Josie said.

Garrett had to choke back a chuckle as Grace's expression clearly said she was not the least surprised. "Well, I'm telling you that Grace, as you can tell from the food here, does it better than all the rest of us put together. She has a real gift."

"And you're on TV?"

Garrett could almost see the wheels turning as Josie tried to figure out how that could benefit her.

"I am." Grace spoke for the first time since Josie had noticed her. "Nice to meet you, Josie."

"So I'll be right there, okay?" Garrett nudged her along, then turned back to Grace once Josie was out of hearing. "Before you start making assumptions, this is strictly business. I have to make nice to everyone here. It's part of the job."

"Did I say anything?" Grace asked, her expression bland.

"You were thinking it."

"So you're reading my mind now?"

"Are we having a fight, Grace?"

"Of course not. What you do is none of my concern." Then her brows snapped together. "Why did you say that about my show? I haven't invited you on."

An idea germinated. "But you should. It would be good for ratings." He waggled his eyebrows. "I'm a hot property."

She rolled her eyes, then glanced over at Josie. "So you seem to believe."

He grinned then. He liked this saucy Grace. "When are you taping?"

"Tonight."

"Perfect. I hate the night before a race, especially a big one. What time shall I be there?"

She huffed out a breath. "Garrett, has it occurred to you that my episodes are planned out to the second? That the food is ordered, that all the camera angles are set out ahead of time?"

"I can just be there and watch. You can teach me for the benefit of your audience. Take pity on me—you know what's in my refrigerator. I should learn to cook."

"You need to be focusing on this race. You told me how crucial it is."

"It is. And I do. But I'm as ready as I'm going to be, and I'll just spend the night pacing. Have mercy on me."

She didn't answer right away. Instead, she studied him. "Garrett, we're as different as night and day. There is no point in spending more time together."

He agreed with her. But. "Have you ever had a fling, Grace?"

Her eyes popped wide. "What?" Then they narrowed. "Garrett Clark," she whispered furiously, "if you think I am just one of your bimbos, you have another think coming. I do not have affairs, and even if I did, it would not be with someone like you." She halted, squeezed her eyes shut, then opened them again. "I'm sorry. I can be a little hot-tempered, but that was unfair. There's nothing wrong with you, for the right woman. That woman just isn't me."

He was surprised to find that she could actually inflict hurt on him. He didn't take women seriously enough for that, as a general rule. He bent close and whispered back. "Fun, darlin'. I think that's a foreign concept for you, but you could use some. That's all I'm proposing, some easy times, a little fun." He shook his head. "Beats the hell out of me why, but I like you, even with that stick up your—" Someone was approaching, so he didn't finish. "Never mind. And forget the show. It was just an idea." He grabbed his plate and stalked off.

He spent the next half hour or so eating and talking, first with Josie and her group, then with others the sponsor and Andrew wanted him to chat up. At last, Andrew announced that Garrett needed his beauty rest and freed him to go.

Only once more did he see Grace, when she herself came to take his empty plate and pressed a piece of paper in his hand he couldn't take the time to read then.

But once outside, he opened it.

And smiled.

Taping at 7:30—be there by 7:00. KRLM Studios.
Wear your uniform.

GRACE HAD NOT BEEN THIS rattled since her first show, on a tiny cable-only channel and filmed in her own catering kitchen for lack of proper facilities at the bare-bones station.

What on earth had she been thinking?

It's not that Garrett misbehaved, either. He was magic on the camera, her producer had already told her, and his charisma was as enticing as his good looks. He took instruction well, was distinctly adorable when he made mistakes, based on the reactions of the audience. He was careful not to get in her way and showed the utmost of respect for her, even praising her food to the high heavens.

But he was just so…there. So bigger-than-life.

Okay, so hot. Ridiculously magnetic and charming and attractive…she could wring his neck. Her concentration was shot, and it was all his fault. Only barely had she averted disaster with the barbecue sauce she'd nearly spilled all over both of them when he got too close and she could feel his warmth and hear him breathe and smell his scent that was so blasted male.

Her producer was signaling, and Grace realized she was supposed to be offering closing remarks, but her head was somewhere else entirely.

"So," she said brightly, too brightly really. "Thanks so much to our guest, driver of the No. 402 Country Bread car for FastMax Racing, Garrett Clark." The audience cheered and clapped so long she had to speak over them. "This is being taped to air before tomorrow's race where I'm sure all of us wish Garrett a great finish. Garrett is, as some of you may know, second in points for the championship and only barely behind Justin Murphy, so it's an important race, with only one left after this." She turned to Garrett and said to him with her eyes as much as her mouth, "Best of luck to you, Garrett."

"Thanks, Grace." Before she could react, he wrapped one strong arm around her waist and dropped a kiss on her lips, then turned to the audience and grinned. "For good luck, you know." When they laughed and cheered louder, he waved to the crowd. "It's been my pleasure, folks, and my thanks to Grace Winters for giving this bachelor hope that he may yet learn to boil water."

The producer signaled that time was up, and all Grace could do was wave goodbye before the camera shut off.

Then, because they hadn't thought to take precautions, Garrett was swallowed up in a sea of fans, and Grace had no opportunity to chew him out for kissing her on national TV.

To be fair, people wanted to talk to her, too, and get autographs, but far too many wanted only to know how it felt to be kissed by the very hot Garrett Clark.

She could kill him. If her children watched this episode, she *would* kill him, she swore. The nerve of the man—

"Excuse me, folks, but I have to let Miss Grace take me to the woodshed now for kissing her without permission." As always, Garrett's charm melted hearts all around, and fond smiles sent them on their way.

She held on to her temper, but only barely. As soon as they found a deserted spot, she turned on him, ready to lash out—

"Have dinner with me back home," he said before she could.

"What? Are you kidding me? After what you did out there?"

"I do declare, Miss Grace," he drawled. "You're even prettier when you're angry. Temper suits you."

She was speechless, no idea where to begin.

"Monday night work for you? We leave early for Homestead this week."

She recovered her voice. "You cannot be serious."

"Why not? We're having fun, right?"

"Go away," she managed. "Before I do something I regret."

"Like lose your temper?" His brown eyes sparkled with golden lights.

"Do not try to charm me, Garrett Clark. I am not one of your bimbos nor an adoring fan."

"I know that," he said quietly. "You are completely unique. You baffle the hell out of me."

"So leave me alone. You'll sleep better at night."

He curled one errant lock of her hair around his finger. "I wish that were true. Unfortunately, I think about you far too often."

"Don't."

A bittersweet smile curved his lips. "Easier said than done." He paused. "Are you really angry about the kiss? I didn't plan to, it just…" He shrugged.

"What, your lips slipped?"

He chuckled. "Yeah, maybe that's it. Grace, it's only dinner. Please. And if it makes you feel better, I never beg women."

"I'm sure you don't have to. Why don't you ask one of your groupies?"

"Because they don't interest me. You do." His expression was completely serious. "I wish you didn't."

Exasperation filled her voice. "This can't go anywhere, Garrett. You're a playboy, and I'm the mother of three kids. I'm probably older than you, anyway."

"I'm thirty-four."

"You don't act like it."

"Ouch. But you're younger, aren't you?"

"I'm thirty-one."

"See? When's your birthday?"

"February twelfth."

"Nearly the right age to be Gina Grosso, and definitely a blonde, but no cigar. Kent had a big birthday party this summer, so obviously you missed the cutoff to qualify."

"That's not funny, Garrett."

"I know. I'm sorry." An awkward pause.

"How about you?"

"July twenty-seventh."

"A Leo—figures."

"Why's that?"

"Showboat, hardheaded—you're the definition of a Leo."

"So what's your point?" he teased.

She had to laugh.

"See? You have fun with me, admit it. I make you laugh. You need more chances to laugh, Grace." He paused. "And, well, I could use the moral support."

She had the feeling she was hearing the real Garrett Clark just then. He was under tremendous pressure, she knew. And it was only a dinner. "If I can get a babysitter. It's a school night, you know."

"Oh. Wow. I don't think about stuff like that."

"That much is obvious." But she found herself smiling at him. "It's only dinner, Garrett. Just between friends."

"Friends with benefits?" The charming scapegrace was back.

"The only benefit you might get, my friend—" she purposely emphasized the word *friend* "—is a home-cooked meal now and again."

"I'll take your home-cooked meal and raise you a goodnight kiss." He lifted her hand to his lips, turned it over and kissed her palm.

She yanked it back and tried very hard to ignore the quick jitter that raced through her body. "I'm not a gambler, Garrett."

His smile was wide and wicked. "That's okay. I am." But he didn't press. Instead, he saluted her and stepped back. "I'll wait until you're done and take you back to your hotel."

"Don't you have a curfew or something?"

"You wish. Nope, I'm all yours, and far too much of a gentleman to let you get back on your own."

"I'm not inviting you up to my room."

"No surprise there, but I'm still going to wait for you."

She shook her head and turned toward the stage.

"Thank you, Grace," he said softly. "I'll race better, thanks to you."

She didn't turn back, but a foolish smile crept over her face.

And a tiny ache crept into her heart.

CHAPTER SIX

SEVENTEEN LAPS TO GO.

"Save me some fuel, Garrett," requested his crew chief, Robbie. "If we pit, we lose, but it's gonna be close."

"How am I supposed to save fuel and stay in front?" Garrett had his hands full, simply swapping leads with Kent Grosso. Grosso couldn't overtake him in the points, but Will Branch in the No. 467 car had been on his tail all day. One wrong move, and Will could.

Garrett had to win. "How's the No. 448 car on fuel?"

"Murphy's close, too," Robbie responded. "Best guess, though, I think he can make it."

Justin Murphy still led in points, yet a win would put Garrett on top, even if Justin finished second. "What about Will?"

"They're nervous, I can tell."

So neither could afford to push to take the lead, not yet. Garrett couldn't afford to assume anything, though. Too many laps left.

"You're getting better times on the high line," Robbie remarked.

"Branch will pass me if I move up. He likes the bottom." Garrett swore silently that he had no options.

"Watch out for the next lapped car. The No. 487 looks wicked loose."

"Which way should I go around him? What's he been doing?"

"I think you—go high, go high," his spotter, Jamie, shouted suddenly. "They're wrecking in front of you, four cars up."

Smoke billowed and cars spun like a toddler's tantrum. Garrett could barely see two feet in front of his hood, then not at all. "Talk to me, Jamie."

"Stay high, stay high—drop low now, there's one next to the wall—"

Garrett swerved, and felt simultaneously the clip from his left rear and a scrape on the right. He battled the car and somehow made it through the debris to emerge—

Second. Will Branch had passed him in the melee.

"Damn it."

"Caution's out, caution's out," intoned his spotter.

"We'll make it up, Garrett. It's only one spot. We can do this," Robbie encouraged.

"I'm hit, left rear and right front. Feels like a tire rub on the left rear."

"Jamie, can you see the damage?" asked Robbie.

"Not yet, but I've asked the No. 502's spotter to tell us what he sees."

Garrett's gut roiled with the knowledge that his edge had just been lost, and he needed the fastest pit stop ever. No time to be banging out fenders. If Will Branch or Justin Murphy did a splash-and-go, it was all over.

"I think the right front is okay, but the left rear took a worse hit."

Damn. "We need a splash 'n go, Robbie," Garrett said.

"You cut a tire, and you'll fall completely out of contention. We've got to pull out the fender, Garrett, and we'd better do a left side while we're at it." His crew chief kept his voice calm, but Garrett knew he had to be furious, too.

Fury wouldn't help, though. Only calm would. "Get me the tires, and guys, do it fast. I'll make up the time." He put conviction he didn't feel into his voice. A win wouldn't come now, not without some disaster for Branch or Murphy. Best he could do was to stay close.

And pray for neither to win.

Anybody else…anybody but one of them.

"Pit road's open," said his spotter.

"Come on in, Garrett. We're gonna do you proud," said his jackman.

"I know you will." Garrett focused intently on his tachometer to get maximum speed down pit road without a penalty. Every fraction of a second counted.

The guys were as good as their word.

"Justin had to take two tires, as well," reported his spotter.

"How about Will?"

"Splash 'n go. Sorry."

"That's okay. Thanks, guys."

"You're sixth off pit road," said Robbie.

Not great, but it was what it was. "Who's ahead of me?"

"O'Bryan first, Grosso second, Branch third, Matheson fourth, Murphy fifth."

"Okay, gang, hold on to your hats."

Once the green flag waved again, Garrett's world narrowed to a sole focus: getting back to the front with nine laps left. Not easy, but not impossible.

Nine laps.

He picked off Justin Murphy coming from the outside of turn four.

By turn two of the next lap, Justin passed him on the inside.

"Who's led the most laps today?" Garrett asked.

"Don't talk, Garrett—drive!" Andrew ordered.

"Tell me about live points and I will." Grimly he focused ahead.

"Justin's got six on you right now."

So Garrett had to finish at least one spot ahead to pull in front of Justin in championship points.

"Eat my dust, Murphy." He darted below, dancing centimeters above the yellow line.

He glanced in the mirror to see if he was pulling away.

"He's closing in, Garrett," said Jamie.

"But his times are better on the high line," said Robbie. "Just like yours."

"Can't let him get under me. Just gotta block. Stay on point, Jamie. I need every bit of warning you can give me."

"You got it. Block high," he said. "Matheson's moving high, too."

Garrett conducted the dance of his life, avoiding running into Zack Matheson only half a car length in front, while moving up and down the track to prevent Justin Murphy from passing him.

"Five laps to go," reported Robbie. "You're doing great, Garrett."

He was driving on pure instinct now, lightning reflexes bypassing conscious thought. Moments like this, when he and the car were one, were as good as it got.

"Will just passed Kent Grosso," reported Jamie. "He's in second."

Second finish over fifth—Will Branch could possibly pass him in the points. "Has he led any laps?"

"No. Shut up and drive," Robbie yelled, in an uncharacteristic show of emotion. "Four laps."

"Grosso's car is fading fast. He's falling down low," said Jamie.

Garrett's gaze shifted toward him for an instant, but it was enough to distract him from Murphy.

"Murphy coming around high…on your bumper, at your quarter…"

Then Garrett's peripheral vision took over as he saw Justin Murphy's car steadily move forward.

"Your front bumper. Clear."

Clear, in this case, was not a positive. Kent Grosso had fallen behind Garrett, but Justin Murphy was now in fourth.

"Three laps." Robbie didn't have to say what they all knew: the window was closing.

Come on, come on, Garrett silently urged his car. *Give me a little more, baby. Just a little more.*

He got right on Justin's bumper, ever vigilant for an opening, but now it was Justin who was blocking every possible chance Garrett had to pass.

"White flag," called his spotter. It was now or never.

Garrett turned the wheel and headed high, a hairbreadth from the wall. *Come on, baby, come on...*

Justin moved right only a fraction, but it was enough—Garrett had no choice but to drop back or hit the wall.

The silence on the radio was deafening. Everyone knew it was too late.

The checkered flag came out. "O'Bryan takes the checkered flag, Branch second, Matheson third, Murphy fourth."

"Points, Robbie. Talk to me." Though he already knew.

"Justin's still in first by eight points. Will has pulled to nine behind you."

So close. Too close. Any of them could still win the championship.

Two of them would lose.

"You can do it, buddy. If it hadn't been for that wreck..."

Robbie was trying to encourage him, but he knew as well as Garrett—and every other team on this track—that *if only* were the two most pathetic words in a driver's vocabulary.

If only got you no championships. *If only* could destroy a team. Close down a shop.

If only meant nothing.

Only winning counted.

I'LL RACE BETTER, THANKS to you, he'd said.

Oh, Garrett... Grace was a crew chief's daughter. She recognized the damage this race had done to Garrett's hopes for a championship.

As she and her crew cleared up in Country Bread's suite after the guests had departed, she thought it was probably better that his appearance here had occurred well before the race and not after. She hadn't liked the attention she'd seen

Mel Springer paying to Will Branch's finish or his scowl when Garrett got into trouble.

He'd recovered brilliantly, had driven his heart out to recoup the spots he'd lost thanks to that wreck, but she'd overheard Springer muttering to the man next to him that Garrett should be more conservative.

She'd wanted to ask him exactly what he thought Garrett could have done differently. The wreck wasn't his fault, and he'd executed nothing less than a miracle making it through the billowing smoke without crashing himself. That he hadn't escaped scot-free was only bad luck.

But, of course, she couldn't interfere. She might be a celebrity chef, but she was still the hired help, and one thing she lectured her people on was not eavesdropping on clients. She hadn't made an effort to listen, but people tended to treat caterers as though they were invisible.

Garrett needed to hear what she'd learned, though.

Or did he?

What would benefit him most, given that he was already under tremendous pressure: to know and be edgy, or not to know and risk being blindsided?

She shouldn't have dinner with him. He needed no distractions in this last week. She should cancel.

If she were to tell him, when would be the best time? How would he be feeling right now? She couldn't help recalling last week, his impromptu nighttime visit. He'd had a troubling race then, yet he'd put aside his worries to comfort her.

FastMax is in trouble. I have to win this championship.

She didn't want to care. She would not let herself get involved.

But Garrett Clark, she was beginning to realize, was so much more than his maverick, playboy image. The least she could do was to warn him. And cancel the dinner, for his sake. There was no future for them, not that she wanted one.

"Grace? We're done here."

She glanced up from her checklist. "Great. Let's head for the plane. Ethan will be tapping his toes, I'm sure."

HE'D RATHER TAKE A BULLET than ride back with his sponsor on the plane right now, but he was committed to do so this week and the next because Andrew had sold Country Bread on how much they'd regret not being on hand as Garrett put down the solid finishes to win the championship.

The four hours back to Charlotte would crawl as the post-mortem played out. He couldn't tug his cap down over his eyes and tune everyone out the way he normally would. He had to suck it up, be charming and supremely confident even though he was discouraged and so tired he thought he might fall asleep walking across the tarmac.

"Garrett?"

He jolted at the sound of Grace's voice. He was so not ready to face her, either, especially since he'd decided while he was showering that he had to cancel their date. He intended to study film and computer readouts until he went blind, to be certain he hadn't missed one tiny bit of information that might garner even a slight advantage at Homestead.

But here she was at the airfield, that beautiful face pinched with concern. "Hey."

"You're going to do fine next week," she said. "What happened wasn't your fault. If you were any less gifted as a driver, you'd have wrecked at least twice in the last ten laps."

He couldn't help it. She just made him feel so good, simply being around her. "Well," he teased. "So much for small talk."

Even in the diminished lights on the airfield, he could see her flush. He reached for her hand. "That wasn't a complaint. Thank you for your faith." He shook his head. "Wish others shared it. My sponsor, for example." He cast a glance at the plane not far away.

"About that…" She pulled her hand away. "Garrett, I heard

something in the suite. Springer was talking about Will Branch, singing his praises."

"Yeah, I know. He thinks Will's a better match." A faint chuckle. "Amazing what marriage and kids can do for the image. Will Branch was wild and undisciplined until he got married."

"I'm sorry. Maybe I shouldn't have said anything, but you said that you're worried about FastMax…." She was wringing her hands.

"No, I needed to hear it. Not that there's any surprise, but I'm about to get on a plane with Springer, and it stands to be a long flight while I get my behind chewed out." He found a smile for her. "Thanks for the warning, Grace. Really."

"We can't go to dinner," she blurted.

It was the damnedest thing. However much he'd been thinking exactly that, hearing her say it wasn't the relief he'd anticipated.

Instead, it actually got his back up, and he reversed himself before he could think. "Why not?"

"Garrett, you must be joking. You can't afford a single distraction. You're in the fight of your life."

She was absolutely right. Everything she was saying made perfect sense.

But there was this hole in the pit of his belly, this gnawing ache that her words had produced. "I know you're right, but—" he heaved a sigh "—I could use something to look forward to at the moment. It's going to be a bitch of a week." He studied her eyes. "You're a distraction, no question. But I feel good when I'm with you, Grace."

"We…maybe we could have dinner later, after the season." Her darting eyes made a lie of that possibility.

Why should he care? Their lives had nothing in common. They had no future. What was the point?

"It's only a meal, as you said. We both have to eat, anyway." He knew he was being stubborn. He didn't care.

"Garrett! Wheels up in two minutes," shouted Andrew. No need to add that being late would not aid Garrett's cause.

"Coming!" Garrett called out before turning back to Grace. "I'll drop by tonight after we get in."

"No. I have a meeting with PR people from my publisher in the morning and two jobs to price out tomorrow. I have to get some sleep." She placed a hand on his arm to soften the refusal. "You must be exhausted." She hesitated for a minute. "All right. On the date—dinner, I mean," she corrected hastily. "If you really think you can spare the time, I'll meet you to save you the drive. Where and when?"

"I'd like to see the kids."

"Daddy will never get them in bed if they see you. Better not."

He was surprised at how disappointed he was. "I always pick up my dates. I'm old-school that way."

"It's not a date, remember?" The look on her face didn't relent.

"All right, come by the race shop, then. Seven-thirty? Go around to the side door and knock. The front will be locked up." He paused. "We'll go someplace casual, no need to dress up."

"See you then. Sleep well, Garrett—and good luck on the ride home."

"Thanks. I have a feeling I'll need it." Despite the scowl likely forming on Andrew's face, Garrett paused just a second longer to watch her walk to the Sanford plane.

And it wasn't only the gentle sway of those hips that held his attention.

You are walking into deep water, son.

He ignored his inner voice and, lighter of heart than he'd been a few minutes before, crossed the tarmac for the possibly endless ride home.

CHAPTER SEVEN

"YO, GARRETT—YOU HAVE a guest," said the FastMax mechanic who answered the side door the next night.

Garrett emerged from a small office where another man and he had obviously been studying a monitor. "Hi." He raked fingers through already-disordered hair. "Sorry, almost done. Marty and I got caught up in something." He seemed distracted.

"Listen, never mind," she said as her misgivings roared back. "You're busy, and I have plenty of work at home." She was halfway into a turn when he grabbed her elbow.

"Grace, don't—" His brow furrowed. "I just…we need to figure out this one thing. It'll only take a minute, I swear."

"You forget I'm the daughter of a crew chief. It's the most crucial week of the race season, and you have a legitimate shot at the championship. I understand, really. Go back inside."

Marty seemed very impatient. Garrett's conflict was apparent. "We'll make it another time. I'm fine, honestly."

He looked into the office, then back at her. "Marty, I'll be back in a second." He wrapped one arm around Grace's waist and all but towed her into an office across the hall, then shut the door behind them. "I am not standing you up, I swear. We're nearly done. If you can give me five minutes, I'll be all yours."

All yours. She stared up into his intent brown gaze as those words sent tiny, inexplicable shivers through her. "It's only dinner, Garrett. We can reschedule. This is your career on the line."

He exhaled, glanced up at the ceiling. Then his gaze captured hers. "I haven't eaten since breakfast. Marty is only humoring me, going through the data for the umpteenth time. I'm driving everyone around here nuts because they'd like to go home. You'll be doing them a favor if you'd just wait a few minutes. They'll probably pick me up bodily and throw me out the door if I force them to work much longer. We're all wired so tight someone's gonna snap before long." There was nothing of the playboy in the man before her. His words might be teasing, but his eyes were dead serious. "Have mercy on all of us, would you?"

His vulnerability touched her. She couldn't seem to help that. She traced her fingers over his jaw and smiled. "All right. I'll sit here, if that's okay. Is this your office?"

"Yeah. Take your time, comb through the drawers for all my dirty little secrets. *Mi casa es su casa.*" He leaned in and gave her a quick kiss. "You may have saved an entire race team from going postal." He walked to the door, then wheeled. "You look hot as hell in those jeans, by the way." He left her gasping for a response.

She did not know what to do with this man. How to deal with how he made her feel.

Deciding that train of thought could be deadly, she instead applied herself to studying what was on the walls. What she found made her smile. Though she knew Garrett had been voted Most Popular Driver more than once, that he'd been a NASCAR Nationwide Series champion and Late Model before that, no trophies or plaques decorated his walls.

There was a surprising lack of anything related to racing on the shelves that lined two walls. Instead, there was a football autographed by Troy Aikman, a plastic figurine of the Tasmanian Devil, a broken hockey stick, a stuffed pheasant, a Rubik's Cube and several stunning nature photos with no photographer's name attributed. One was a black and white of the desert that would have done Ansel Adams proud, another was taken from the peak of a mountain, two were inside a cave and—this was the most surprising—three were close-ups of what she realized were flowers, of all things, only they were so stylized that recognizing the origin of the image required a second.

She had one in her hand, marveling at how the photographer had taken something so ordinary—a tulip blossom—and rendered it nearly an abstract. The knob turned behind her, and she hastened to return the photo to the shelf before facing the door.

"Who did these?"

He shrugged. "Me."

"You?"

"You don't have to sound so astonished." Garrett glanced from her to the photo and back.

"I'm sorry. I didn't look through your desk—I would never do that—but I saw these and…are you okay?"

He nodded, but his weariness was evident.

"Garrett, we don't have to do this, seriously. You're exhausted. Did you sleep at all last night?"

"Some."

"Was the flight back bad?"

His lips quirked. "You might say that."

She went to him. "Be sensible. Don't push yourself any harder. This week is too critical."

"Yeah." He looked away, but there was something about him that reminded her of Matthew when he was trying his hardest not to show his disappointment.

She was not Garrett's mother, nor did she want to be, but she was concerned about him. "Okay, let's try this. Your refrigerator is still bare, right?" She shook her head and grinned. "Why am I asking? You're a bachelor and a driver."

"Hey, I resemble that remark."

"Do you own a single skillet or—never mind. Come on."

She held out a hand, and this time it was she who towed him down the hall and outside. "Get in my car."

He skidded to a halt. "That's a minivan."

"So?"

"I, uh…why would anyone drive one?"

"I'm a mother, Garrett, with three children. Minivans were created with me in mind."

"But—"

"What?" She cocked an eyebrow. "Your masculinity will be threatened by riding in one?"

"Well…yeah. Goes without saying."

She resisted the grin that threatened. "Deal with it. You have no business driving when you're this tired."

"Only if I can watch a Disney movie in the backseat."

He really was too charming by half. "There's a princess movie in the DVD player, but Bella will never forgive you for watching without her."

"Can't have that." Still he hesitated outside.

"Get in, Garrett."

"Yes, ma'am." His salute was cocky, as she'd expect, but it was just a little slower than usual, she was almost certain. "Where are we going?"

"Your place, with a detour first to my shop." When his eyebrows rose, she sent him a quelling glare. "I'm cooking you dinner, and that's that. You're going to eat a good meal, then you're going to bed." At his quick grin, she narrowed her eyes. "Alone. There must be someone on your team who'll retrieve your car for you, right?"

He nodded. "But—"

"No buts. You have to be at your best for Homestead, and that does not include straining your eyes or wrecking your health between now and then. You are one of the best drivers in the world, and you can win this race and the championship, but you can't do either if you don't take care of yourself." At his silence, she glanced over. "Questions?"

"Wouldn't dream of it." Ostentatiously he clamped his open mouth shut. "Ma'am," he added.

She couldn't help the curve of her lips. Blast him, he could no more stop being charming than quit breathing. But a short "Good" was all she replied as they drove into the night.

She turned on the radio to cover the nerves she felt. When she pulled up at the headquarters of Gourmet by Grace and glanced over, she realized he was fast asleep.

The urge she had to stroke his hair was not one iota maternal.

But it was far too fond for her comfort.

IT WAS THE DAMNEDEST THING. An apron should not be sexy. Tied around Grace's waist, however, and drawing his eye to the curve of her hips, it was, oh, it definitely was. Just as watching her bustle around the kitchen, where he most often opened takeout, was a revelation.

"You do not even own a dish towel," she scolded. "Garrett, you're a grown man. There is no excuse."

"Hey, paper towels work, and less laundry."

The look she gave him would have made a weaker man quail. "How are you even still standing, much less able to drive, when you treat your body this way?"

"I work out," he defended.

The color that rose as her gaze moved over his body was a very encouraging sign. She turned away quickly. "Youth will make up for a lot." She brandished a wicked-looking knife at him. "But that won't last. I have to teach you to cook. This is shameful." She clucked her tongue as she magically turned vegetables into piles of colorful slices.

"I'm more of a meat and potatoes guy," he said, eyeing the lack of either.

"Of course you are," she replied drolly. "As in barbecue, hamburgers, steaks slapped on a grill."

"Hey, I grill a mean steak. As a matter of fact, I could do that and save you the trouble...."

Another glare from her. Another gleaming slice of steel. "You think you don't like vegetables, right?" She didn't wait for him to answer. "You haven't had these vegetables. Anyway, you'll get your meat, just hold your horses. You'll have whole grains and vegetables, too, and your body will thank me," she said as she chopped.

His body wasn't focusing on food right now, even though the condo was filling with amazing aromas. With her hair caught up in some kind of clip, a few strands escaping to curl on her slender nape, Garrett stared at that expanse of pale skin and felt a powerful urge to graze it with his teeth, tantalize with his tongue. To turn her around in his arms and press that amazing body against his and—

"—hot?" Grace asked.

He dragged himself out of the fantasy. "What?"

"Do you like things hot, I said."

If his body had been aching before, he'd shot straight to making-a-grown-man-beg now. He took a step toward her before the confusion in her eyes yanked him to the realization that she was talking about food.

He didn't care. "Oh. Uh, yeah."

If he'd thought her beautiful before, sexy before, the answering heat in her eyes shot him into the red zone. He covered the distance between them in quick strides.

"Garrett," she protested weakly.

But when he swept her into his arms and put his mouth on hers in a manner that was far beyond friends, she sank against him with a little catch in her breathing.

After that, he was pretty much toast.

And when she responded in kind, the entire building could have burned down around him, for all he cared.

Suddenly, she tore herself away. "The garlic will scorch." She faced the stove, and for a second, she gripped the counter edge with both hands.

He was a little rattled himself. "Grace—"

"Don't talk to me, not right now, Garrett. Please." A quick glance from her showed him that she was shaken, too. "I can't cook if I can't concentrate."

"We can order in. Come here."

She brandished the huge knife again. "Get...back. Keep those hands to yourself." Her pupils were huge and dark, and she kept returning her gaze to his lips, whatever her logic might be trying to tell her. "I am feeding you first."

His brows lifted. "And after?"

Her own snapped together. "I plan to stuff you so full that you'll have nothing but sleep on your mind."

"Oh, bed is there already." He grinned.

"Sleep, Garrett. Alone," she added.

"We'll see." Cheered by her desperation, he settled back against the counter, arms folded, to watch. "So, Teach, show me what you got."

"Go away." Pretty color stained her cheeks again.

He tucked one strand behind her ear, bending close so that she'd feel his breath on her throat. "Not a chance."

No knife brandishing now. Only Grace taking an unsteady breath, then trying to ignore him.

Oh, yeah. He did like things hot.

And from her reactions, tonight and before, he had the feeling he'd barely begun to tap the passion bubbling beneath the surface of the very lovely, usually composed, bossy but warm and kind Grace Winters.

Who was, at this moment, no more in control than he was.

And who was getting more interesting by the day.

"How are the kids?" Garrett asked. "This is amazing, by the way." He forked up another mouthful and made quick work of it.

"Even if there are veggies?"

His eyes crinkled. "I have this sneaking suspicion everything on my plate is good for me."

She grinned back. "Don't let that stop you."

"Are you kidding? Nobody better get between me and this food."

"It's not a fancy meal, but since you haven't eaten all day, I thought quicker was better."

His gaze lit. Dropped to her lips. "Sometimes."

"Stop that." But she couldn't totally regret the flutter low in her belly. She hadn't been with a man since Todd's accident, and sometimes, in the crush of raising kids and running her business, she wondered if that part of her might have died. It was reassuring, if not altogether comfortable, to discover that she'd been wrong.

At least in the presence of Garrett Clark, whose smile was sinfully beautiful…and off-limits.

Or should be.

She grasped at his earlier question about how the kids were doing to defuse the sexual tension that hadn't abated since that kiss. "Bella has decided her Barbie dolls need a race car. Unfortunately, she chose Matthew's and crashed it into a vase I loved."

"Uh-oh." He laughed. "That girl is something, I swear."

"Oh yes…like perhaps what will send me to the asylum before she hits first grade."

"I like her."

"I'm sure Matthew would gladly give her to you. It wasn't only the vase that suffered damage."

"I'll get him another."

"No. Bella will have to do that."

"But she's only four. She won't have the money."

"She can work for it. And she's nearly five."

"Work for it? Grace, she's too little, and anyway, I'd like to."

"I'm not selling her to slave labor, Garrett. She isn't too young to learn to take responsibility. She will feed Tomi, and she'll gather up newspapers for recycling, things like that. Of course, she'll make a mess while she's doing it, and it would be much easier to do those tasks myself, but that doesn't teach her a lesson."

"She's just a baby, Grace." His expression was pained. "I've got plenty of money to replace the car."

"Much as I love Bella, she has the potential to turn into a monster because she's so hardheaded. Her saving grace is that her heart is huge, but she gets so intent on her own way that she can run roughshod over others. Everyone in our house has to pitch in, and I would have started her on these tasks soon, anyway. She already is responsible for making her own bed and brushing Tomi."

"Wow," he said. "Good thing I never wanted children. You're tough, Grace."

She stiffened. "I love my children."

"I didn't say otherwise. All I meant was that you have discipline, that you don't take the easy way out. Me, I'd be buying them stuff and probably feeding them crap. I'd be a lousy parent." He looked up at her. "You're really good at this."

"I have no choice. I'm all they have." And just like that, any foolish notions she might have toyed with evaporated. *I never wanted children.* They really did not have anything in common.

"How's Millie? Do you think it bothers her that Bella steals the show so often? I mean, she's great—so sweet and soft, and she makes me want to wrap her up and protect her."

And then he goes and says something like that, and I know he could be a great father, despite what he believes. Grace shook her head and rose to clear the table, weary of the confusion.

Garrett grabbed her arm. "You cooked, I clean up. Sit down and talk to me while I finish."

"I need to go, Garrett."

"What? Why? Did I say something? I—is it wrong to want to protect Millie?"

She stared at him. He didn't understand, couldn't, not when he had no children, no huge responsibility that some days weighed too heavily on her. It wasn't his fault that he didn't get it. "She's okay. She took her unicorn to show-and-tell last Friday."

His smile was its own sun. "Thanks. That makes me feel great." He hesitated. "Grace, I'm so sorry I scared her. I have no idea what I was thinking. Sarah's a fun girl, but she's not... Oh, hell, I don't know why I was even there."

Watching his earnest confusion, she thought he really might not. She'd married young, and she'd never had the chance to be single and foolish and footloose. She might have acted exactly like Sarah, especially faced with a man as magnetic as Garrett. "Our lives are different, that's all. I've been married and a mother since I was twenty-two."

"A girl yourself," he observed. "Did you—had you known him a long time?"

"I can't remember when I didn't. We grew up next door to each other. He's—he was six years older and thought I was just a pesky little kid."

"Obviously that changed."

"When I was in high school, he came back home after finishing college. I looked different. I wasn't the scrawny little girl anymore."

His gaze warmed as it ranged over her body. "I'll vouch for that."

She ducked her head. "Well, anyway, it was like we'd never met before. I fell madly in love. I would have married him the day I graduated—sooner, really—but our parents insisted I go to college, and Todd agreed." Her head rose. "I confounded them all. I went to culinary training instead." Her smile widened, remembering. "That was only a two-year program."

"You really loved him."

Hearing that past tense stung. "A part of me always will."

"He was a lucky guy. I envy him." Garrett's eyes were brown, as Todd's had been, but Garrett's sometimes glowed golden.

It disturbed Grace greatly that she had trouble recalling the exact shade of Todd's. "I really should go." She rose again.

This time he rose with her. "I'm sorry. I'm not trying to be insensitive, honest. Is it not okay to talk about him?"

"No, it's all right, it's just that—" She pressed her lips together. "I don't—I haven't—" She picked up her plate and his and escaped to the small kitchen. "I'm out of practice, Garrett," she said with her back to him. "And I was never a good flirt. There was only ever Todd, you see, and…" Her voice shook a little.

His hand wrapped around her upper arm and turned her gently. "I won't hurt you, Grace," he said solemnly. "You confuse me, too, you know. I can't seem to get my footing around you."

"You? Mr. World-Class Playboy?"

His face tightened. "That's my rep. It's not me."

"You forget—I've seen you in a utility closet." Why was she doing this, shoving him away as fast and hard as possible?

"I thought that was a closed topic." He clasped her other arm and drew her close. "Grace, you're different. You're something special, something rare."

However touched she might be, she couldn't forget that she had other responsibilities that had to take precedence. Not for one second could she let go of the fact that she was the only parent three children possessed. "We have almost nothing in common, Garrett. We've established that. It's okay. You're a single man in a high-profile profession. You have freedoms I don't, and that's all right. I don't really want them. I like my life. My children are my focus, and I have a lot of other balls to juggle." She cast him a bright smile. "I'd like to be friends, though, I truly would. I enjoy your company. We can have dinner from time to time, if you'd like—"

"Give me this week," he interrupted.

"What?"

"Are you going to Homestead?"

"Yes, but what does that have to do with anything?"

"Come with me. Stay with me. Give me this one week— hell, call it charity if you want."

"Why?" She was honestly baffled at the swift change of topic.

He let her go, began to pace. Raked one hand through his hair. Whirled and stared accusingly at her. "You confuse the hell out of me, you know that? I mean, you distract me and yet you settle me. I feel better with you, way better than without you, and you haven't even let me take you to bed."

She opened her mouth to argue, but he held up a hand. "I don't get it. Yes, you're sexy as hell, and you make my teeth ache I want you so bad sometimes, but I also like simply being with you, talking with you, shoot, even arguing with you." He frowned. "I never argue with women." Then he grinned. "And I spend precious little time talking."

She couldn't help her laugh. "So I'm supposed to, what, be your unicorn?"

A flash of white teeth. "Maybe."

She wished he weren't so irresistible. "I'm not staying with you, Garrett. I have a reputation to consider. I will not shame my children, even if they're too little to understand. Their mother does not shack up."

"It wouldn't be shacking up."

"Oh? And exactly what would you call it?"

He threw up his hands. "I just—Grace, this is going to be a very difficult week, so shoot me for wanting to have you where I could get my hands on you easily."

"Excuse me?"

"I mean—oh, hell, you get me all tangled up. I don't mean that disrespectfully or gratuitously or anything. I just—I'd like to be able to spend time with you when you have it, but we'll both have precious little free time this week." He stared at her, his eyes more naked than she'd ever seen them. "All I meant was that if we were staying together, we could at least have time last thing at night and first thing in the morning."

"And in between?" she asked with an arch of her brow.

"Okay, so sue me. I'd love to get you in my bed, but I'd understand—"

"Garrett, we barely know each other. The fact that you'd expect me to shack up with you for a week demonstrates that quite clearly."

"Stop calling it that. Okay, you're right. I get it. And I meant no offense, I just—" This smile was charming but mostly because he was so frustrated that he was making mistakes. "Can we start over?"

She watched him, as astonished by how much she wished she could stay with him as by the very fact that he'd asked. "What is it you really want, Garrett?"

His eyes bored into her. "You."

Her insides shivered. "For a week?"

He never glanced away. "For a start."

"One week only. After Homestead, we go our separate ways. I will not stay with you, but I'll do my best to reserve my spare time for you. The kids will be at home with Daddy and Hope, so that will make things easier."

"I wish they'd be there to see me win," he said, and the fleeting wistfulness on his features grabbed a dangerous hold on her heart.

"I'm not misleading them to think there's anything between us but friendship. They're young, and they miss having a father."

"And I'd be a lousy one." An odd expression rose.

"Maybe you're wrong about that."

"I assure you I'm not." He looked up. "I was never sorry about that before."

She would not touch that topic with a ten-foot pole. "Garrett…"

"It's okay, Grace. Never mind. My idea was a bad one. You're a forever kind of woman, and I'm a temporary man, at best. You deserve better." This time it was he who turned away and began cleaning up the kitchen.

Grace watched him with a curious ache in her heart. For the life of her, she could not seem to fit Garrett Clark into any neat little box. Every time she tried, some new tendril escaped. He was a complicated man, more so with every minute she spent in his company.

"I—I'll see you in Homestead. I arrive on Thursday." She picked up her purse and readied herself to escape like the coward she was, but this was the best she could offer at the moment.

He kept his back to her, though his hands stopped moving.

"Give me your cell number," she said, scribbling her own on a paper towel at hand. "Here's mine. Call me whenever you have time this week, all right?" So it wasn't exactly what he'd asked—why did she have this sick feeling in her chest?

At last he turned. Stared at her for a long time.

"Please, Garrett. I'm doing the best I can here."

His broad shoulders eased a little. At last he rattled off a series of numbers.

With shaking hands, she wrote them on the paper towel and tore off the piece. "Good night, Garrett. Please…sleep. I'll cook you a good meal when I get there Thursday, all right?"

His expression made it clear that food was not what he wanted from her, but all he said was "Thanks."

Feeling a powerful need to apologize, Grace turned on wobbly legs and left.

Before she gave in and stayed.

And expected too much from a man who'd given her ample warning.

CHAPTER EIGHT

"GARRETT? IT'S GRACE."

"Hey, there." He sat up from where he was slumped on the sofa, flipping channels. After the way they'd parted the night before, he wouldn't have bet a plugged nickel on hearing from her. "What's up?"

"Oh…" Her voice was a little tentative. "Not much. Just…working. You?"

She'd seemed inclined to keep her distance until she arrived in town when she'd left Monday night. He wondered what had changed her mind. "Well, let's see…I've shaken approximately four thousand three hundred eighty-seven hands, kissed a couple of dozen babies, and my most notable autograph surface so far is the top of an old man's head."

"You're kidding." Then she giggled. "Really?"

"I kid you not. Scout's honor." The sound of her amusement warmed him as nothing had since she'd walked out of his condo. "Want to know why?"

"I'm afraid to ask."

"He didn't want to mess up his brand-new Kent Grosso cap. Or his Dean Grosso shirt."

"Oh, Garrett, I'm sorry."

He chuckled. "Don't be. He was pretty cool about it. Said I wasn't his driver, but he'd take a picture of his dome for his grandson who is a big fan. Not that his grandson had a lick of sense, he hastened to add." He laughed again. "Old guy was a pip. Ninety if he was a day, I swear. Kinda reminds me of

Milo." At the thought of the patriarch of the Grosso clan, he smiled. "Milo tells it like he sees it, every time." Then her situation struck him. "Oh. Sorry."

"No, that's okay. I like Milo, too. He's like the grandfather kids wish for. I never knew any of my grandparents."

"Me, neither." He paused. "Is it okay to ask if you all have heard anything…about your mom, I mean? Or would you rather not talk about it?"

"I don't mind that you asked. The family's reactions are all different. Daddy's mostly stoic, and Ethan and Jared are still furious. No one wants to discuss the subject but Hope. She worries about Daddy, and so do I. But no, to answer your question, nothing's turned up, really…"

"What does *nothing really* mean?"

A heartfelt sigh. "There is one thing, but it doesn't exactly help. Ethan heard from Jake McMasters that he and that detective Lucas Haines believe they're close to identifying the woman who was Gina Grosso."

"Wow. Do Patsy and Dean know?"

"Jake says no. He told Ethan that he and Haines don't want to put them through any more until there's absolute proof."

"Such as?"

"Beats me. DNA, I guess, but doesn't that take time?"

"Not my area of expertise."

"Mine, either." She fell silent.

He found himself unusually patient. Just hearing her voice was the best thing that had happened to him all day.

"I hate that my family's being dragged into this, even if Susan turns out to be wrong. But at the same time, I can't help feeling really sorry for the Grossos when I consider what it would be like if Millie or Matthew or Bella had gone missing. That would kill me."

"Gina Grosso was only a day or two old, though, right? They didn't know her the way you do your children."

"It wouldn't matter. That bond begins the second you lay

eyes on them—much earlier, actually. The first time you feel your baby move. You begin to get a sense of the personality early on. To go through nine months, to hold that child in your arms and then to lose her…and worse, to have no idea where she is…" Her breath hitched. "And to be told your baby is dead and to have to live your life not knowing if she was afraid or cold or hungry—" A choked sob was the only sound.

"Grace…" He felt helpless, being this many miles apart. He didn't like the feeling one damn bit.

"I'm sorry." She sniffed. "I admire Patsy, and my heart breaks for her. To go through all that, then to find out years later that you'd missed your child's entire life… Garrett, I can't believe my mother would do such a horrible, evil thing. But if she did—" her voice wobbled, and she went silent for a moment, then cleared her throat "—then she wasn't the woman I believed she was, and I'm left with no mother at all. She's all I had. My only real family. I'm sorry—I should go."

"Don't hang up, Grace. You stay with me, you hear?" A fierce desire to protect her, to shelter her, swept through him like a storm. "Damn, I wish you were here."

"Me, too," she said so softly he wasn't sure he heard right. "That's why I called, because I'm coming down on Wednesday instead, and I know you're there for sponsor events but I wondered…"

"Who are you flying with? Tell me what time, and I'll be there to pick you up."

"You don't have to."

"Grace." He didn't let her finish. "What time will you be here? Whose plane are you coming on?"

"I'm flying commercial." She gave him the information.

"I'll be there."

"I know you have a lot—"

"I'll be there. And Grace?"

"What?"

"People are complicated. Life is complicated. I'm not

saying your mother was guilty of the accusation, but even if she was, the way she raised you and loved you, that has to count for something. She gave you a safe, stable place to grow up, and trust me, I know from experience that steadiness cannot be overrated. She devoted herself to her family, and there's no question you all turned out well. You can't discount that."

A long silence, then another sniff. "I guess not." Another pause. "Thank you."

"I'm glad you called." The man who'd avoided entanglements for thirty-four years realized he really was. What an eye-opener.

"Me, too. Garrett, I'm sorry about last night. I didn't—it wasn't…" Her voice trailed off.

He understood. There was too much to say, and he was lousy with words, anyway. "Just get down here, okay? I'll see you tomorrow at three-thirty."

"But if something comes up," she began.

"It won't." No matter what.

Even if he had absolutely no idea where whatever this was between them was going.

"Sweet dreams, Grace."

"'Night, Garrett."

Still, it was a few seconds before either of them disconnected.

He waited for her to do it. Then he began punching numbers into his phone and kicked off the process of rearranging his very crowded day.

GRACE WALKED OFF THE PLANE, already regretting her phone call of the night before. She'd nearly contacted him to cancel several times before her plane took off.

Yet she hadn't. If only she knew why.

Suddenly she spotted him, and however unwise she knew it to be, she was glad.

"Great disguise," she said.

He grabbed her carry-on, then pulled the collar of his WWE jacket up and the bill of his Dallas Cowboys cap lower, adjusted his sunglasses. "I thought about a Groucho nose and glasses or maybe a clown wig, but no one at the track had either. I borrowed the jacket from my hauler driver. I was hoping to save your reputation."

"I'm not sure it's working." She nodded to a couple nearby who were excitedly pointing and arguing. A young woman raised a camera.

"Walk fast." He reached for her hand and all but towed her.

Breathless and amused by the adventure of being on the lam, Grace raced to keep up with his long legs, and somehow they made it through the airport without incident. When they got to the parking garage and he used the remote to unlock the vehicle, she burst out laughing at the sight of it. "Want me to drive?"

He appeared more than a little disgruntled as he scanned the minivan. "It's all I could scare up on short notice. It belongs to one of the ladies in the front office at the track." He shrugged. "Anyway, it's good for disguise, too."

"Oh, but if reporters catch you in it, your rep will never be the same."

"Not very nice to be so amused, you know." He opened her door for her.

She glanced back at him, ready with a smart-aleck remark, but he was standing so close. He was suddenly very real…on an all new level. Any attempt at sarcasm fled in the face of her confusion.

He removed his sunglasses. "I'm glad you're here." He touched her cheek.

To no one's surprise more than her own, she allowed herself to lean into his hand just a little. "Me, too. Though it makes no sense, you realize, and—"

"Shh." He laid his fingers on her lips. "I don't care why you're here. Could we just let logic go for a few days? Would it kill either of us?"

Maybe, she wanted to respond. *Because I'm scared of how you make me feel.* But his open gaze spoke to her. Called out to something she didn't want to think about too much just yet. She was always responsible. Was it so wrong not to be, just for now?

Not if you're willing to pay the price when all this ends, wisdom reminded her.

So what? It wasn't as if she hadn't been through tough times before. She'd handle what she had to. "I guess we'll see," she responded, going for insouciance, however uncharacteristic of her that might be.

His smile wasn't his usual cocky one, either. "I guess we will." He lowered his head and, before she could react, brushed his mouth over hers.

Inside, she shivered. Hesitated…then kissed him back.

His hand slid into her hair and held her while he proceeded to wreak maximum havoc with her equilibrium. Grace's whole body lit with anticipation, with appreciation, with…oh, lordy, the man could kiss, could drive her crazy with only his lips.

Slowly he drew away, though he didn't go far. His eyes locked on hers. "I don't know what this is, either, but don't assume this is a normal experience for me, Grace. You should know that. I've never known a woman like you. I want to be careful with you." He stared at her for endless seconds. "I wish…" He shook his head.

Something powerful pulsed between them. Whatever she'd thought initially about Garrett Clark, she understood now that he was far more complex than his image. That he was a fierce competitor who was also a thoroughly decent man. He would not relish hurting her; she believed that.

But he would. And she had to be willing to pay that price, walking in.

She wasn't that experienced with men, but she had a lot of practice at handling what life could dish out. She'd survived losing her husband at twenty-eight and having to go on with three small and devastated children. She'd handled losing her mother far too early. She'd found a way to deal with being left with a mountain of debt and children who would need college one day, plus shoes and food and so much else in the meantime, and she'd managed to make a life for all of them while keeping the wolf from the door.

She'd survive Garrett Clark.

But for the next few days, she began to consider the notion that perhaps she could afford to stop thinking so much and just enjoy whatever pleasure they might share. Garrett had his own pressures, his own responsibilities, and gnawing at the bone of *what-if* or *if-only* would help neither of them.

"Let's make a pledge," she proposed. "Whatever time we can manage together from now until Sunday's over, we'll lighten up and just have fun."

"You think you can manage that, Miss Grace?"

She cocked her head. "Can you, Mr. Playboy?" She grinned to let him know she was teasing.

His features eased. "Hey, I'm all about fun, you know that." If worry still haunted his eyes, she resolved to do her best to take that away, too. For both their sakes.

"I'm counting on it. Okay, so I'm starving. I missed lunch. Where's a grocery?"

"Uh-uh." He closed her door and rounded the vehicle. "You aren't spending your off-time feeding me this week." He closed his own door, buckled up and started the engine. "How do you feel about Cuban food?"

"I feel good." She realized that though she definitely needed practice in lightening up, she actually was hopeful and optimistic.

He pulled out of the parking spot, then hesitated. Looked at her. "I'm really glad you're here, Grace."

She smiled back. "So am I."

He shifted the transmission and took off. "Even if I have to drive a minivan," he muttered.

Her laughter needed no practice just then.

DINNER WAS FUN, AND, better yet, private. He'd found the little hole-in-the-wall a few years ago, and the owners had taken pity on him when his food had gone cold the first time because he was too busy signing autographs. Now they provided him with a booth that was set off from the other diners and with its high back he could remain incognito.

He'd never been so glad as tonight. Grace had been as good as her word, keeping the atmosphere light and free. He couldn't help wondering what would have happened if he'd met her long ago, before life had thrown so much at her.

When the waiter returned with the check, she glanced at her watch. "I should try Ethan soon. Daddy thought he was coming down today, too."

"So why didn't you fly down with him?"

She glanced to the side, then at him. "Because I wasn't sure I wanted a watchdog."

Everything in him went still. "I've been trying not to ask where you're staying."

She plucked her phone from her purse but didn't use it. "I couldn't get my hotel a night earlier."

"You know there's an easy solution," he said.

She lifted her gaze slowly. "I do." White teeth bit into her full lower lip. "I told Daddy I had a friend down here who'd put me up."

He'd been maybe fifteen the last time his body felt this electrified by possibility. "Not that many people are in town yet, though that'll change tomorrow." He kept his gaze on hers. "My motor home is parked on a curve of the lake. Right now, there's no one on either side for a few spaces."

"Garrett, I don't…" She shook her head. "I don't like sneaking around."

"We've been doing it ever since you arrived."

"But that's different." Her lashes swept down.

He reached across the table for the hand that was crumpling her napkin. "I'm sorry."

"For what?"

He stared into those big blue eyes that claimed more and more of his dream time. "That my reputation is so bad that you're uncomfortable being seen with me." He was surprised at how true it was.

"I am such a coward. I don't admire that one bit." Before his eyes, she straightened her shoulders and tossed her hair. Took a deep breath and looked him in the eye. "I am a grown woman. Just because I haven't been with anyone but my…" She pressed her lips together. "Because I've only been with one man is no excuse."

He had to close his own eyes for a second to gather himself. "Do you know how impossibly erotic that is? Or how terrifying?"

"You? How could you be afraid? You've been with so many women."

His chuckle was sheer rue. "I never expected to be ashamed of my track record, but damned if I'm not." He couldn't help his frown. "You are not a comfortable woman to be with sometimes, Grace. I can't say that it's all that much fun to be forced to reexamine your whole life."

"Then don't." She yanked her hand back and scooted to the edge of the booth, lifting her cell into better light in preparation to dial. "I'll find a room."

He rose swiftly and grabbed the phone. She gasped in outrage, but he held it out of her reach. "I said it wasn't always fun. I never said it wasn't high time I did it."

"You're not that easy to deal with, either, you know."

"Good." He tucked the phone in his pocket, threw some bills on the table and slid his arm around her waist. "Maybe we've both been too comfortable until now."

"Garrett Clark," she muttered, "keep your hands off me."

"I've barely gotten them on you," he retorted as he towed her out of the café, nodding to the owners as they left. Hernando and Marina looked vastly entertained.

As would most everyone who'd ever known him. Garrett Clark had women fawning all over him, not pushing him away. Some might say it was his just deserts. He would do better not to respond, since whatever he said would not be meant for polite company.

At last they were in the parking lot. Instead of going straight to that blasted minivan, he detoured her into a shadowed corner. There he whirled her back against a stucco wall, and when her mouth opened no doubt to lambaste him, he gave her something else to focus on.

He poured his confusion and shame and, damn it, yes, a taste of his fury into a kiss that might or might not be curling her toes.

But it was damn sure curling his.

In an instant, his misery fled at the taste of a very different Grace, not careful now, not hesitant, but fiery and demanding as he had only dreamed her before. He responded, his own desire rising higher, straining toward her as the only possible source of what he'd been missing for so long....

She tore her mouth from his, and it was all he could do not to drag her back. "I didn't have to be here until tomorrow," she said.

"What? What?" So caught in craving, he didn't understand at first. "What did you say?"

She gripped the lapels of his jacket. "I said I just defied everything I thought I knew about myself, and I came down here to be with you tonight, Garrett Clark. So are you going to take me to your bed or are we going to waste more time arguing?"

If he'd thought his body was at fever pitch before, it was nothing—*nothing*—compared to how he felt right now. "You do drive me insane, Miss Grace." He pressed a hard kiss to her mouth.

Then he circled her waist with one arm and covered ground toward the car as fast as his legs would carry him.

While the blasted woman cruised her mouth down his jaw and over his throat.

In between small spurts of wicked laughter.

GRACE WASN'T SURE WHO this woman was.

But she kinda liked her.

Oh, of course there would be a reckoning—life always demanded one—but right now, she was doing pretty well at shoving that inevitability way into the back of her mind.

She was crazy, surely. Gone over the edge, no doubt.

But Garrett's mouth…the wandering fingers that even now were driving her insane as they trailed over her knee and…

"Why is this console so big?" he muttered.

Even as she shivered, she couldn't help smiling in delight. Grace Hunt Winters, a wanton woman, driving a man crazy. Who would ever have dreamed it?

"I'd ask what that smile's about, but I like the look of it too much to spoil it," Garrett said as they rolled up to the security gate at the track. He withdrew his hands and lowered the window. "Evening, Bill."

"Hi, Mr. Clark. Not much longer to wait." The guard glanced around him toward Grace, and Garrett could almost feel her shrinking.

If Bill only knew. Garrett felt as if he'd been waiting for this night for far longer than he'd actually known Grace. "I'm ready." He couldn't help his grin at the double entendre.

"Well, good luck to you. Watch out for that Murphy. He managed to marry that Grosso girl despite their family feud. He's a sneaky one. Can't be too careful."

"I'll take that to heart, Bill, I promise. I'll be real careful." Garrett heard a little snort from the passenger seat and couldn't help his own grin. "See you later."

Bill saluted. "Sure thing, Mr. Clark."

Garrett drove through the gate slowly enough to lend credence to his promise of caution, even though he wanted to punch the gas. "Not very nice," he said to Grace.

When he glanced over, she was fighting a smile. "*Careful* isn't exactly your middle name." She faced him. "Come to think of it, what is your middle name?"

"I don't have one." Now.

"Seriously? I thought everyone did."

"What's yours?"

"Grace."

"So what's your first name?"

"We don't know each other that well." Her droll tone made him smile.

"C'mon, it can't be that bad."

"Easy for you to say."

"Really? It's that terrible?" Suddenly he had to know. "Okay, Elvis."

"Wow…okay, it's not that bad."

He was surprised not to be flinching from the naked truth. "No, I mean that's my middle name. Was. I changed it as soon as I was legal."

She laughed out loud, then clapped her hand over her mouth. "Sorry. Your mother was a fan, I guess?"

"You might say that. If you remember that fan came from the word *fanatic*."

"Seriously?"

"Oh, yeah. My mother might not have been much for staying with one man, but that was because Elvis held her heart. She swore she'd gone out with him once."

"You don't believe it?"

He couldn't keep all the bitterness from his tone. "My mother was never one to inspire faith of any kind."

"I'm sorry. She's dead?"

"Probably not. I have no idea. She moved on once I had a choice and went back to live with Andrew."

"Garrett…" She put her hand on top of his and squeezed. "That's inexcusable."

"That's my mother." He parked the minivan outside the gate to the drivers' and owners' lot where he'd promised to leave it for Annette, the assistant to the track owner. He helped Grace from the passenger side and retrieved her bag, then handed the keys to the guard with a few words of direction. "We walk from here. Hope that's okay."

"Sure." Obviously distressed by what she'd heard, Grace walked right past the guard without cringing at all over being seen.

Garrett cursed himself for ruining the mood. "Don't worry about it, Grace. It's old news."

She turned in front of him, forced him to halt. "What she did was despicable. I'd like to give her a piece of my mind."

"And that—" he kissed the tip of her nose "—is why your children are very, very lucky." Then he drew her into his side and started walking again.

When they reached his motor home, he was more glad than ever that he'd given his driver the night off, in hopes there would be a need for privacy. He unlocked the door, which activated a set of low lights, then gestured her up the steps. "After you, madam." He followed her in.

She stood only a few feet from the door, studying the interior, and he tried to see it through her eyes. He'd straightened up the mess before he'd gone to pick her up at the airport, thank goodness. This motor home was not new, but it was new to him this season, the first one he'd ever owned. FastMax had had too many lean years to be splurging on motor mansions like some of the other drivers had.

She turned to him, her eyes big and dark and a little uneasy. Before he could apologize again for wrecking the mood, she smiled. "I don't know what I expected, exactly. Ethan's place is always the height of order, but Jared is a slob, through and through. He saves all his organization for building engines."

He relaxed a little. "Probably you thought there'd be piles of beer cans, with girlie magazines and game controllers and pizza boxes scattered around."

The corners of her eyes tilted up. "And were there before you cleaned up?"

"No girlie magazines and no beer cans, not this week." He shrugged. "Hey, I figure pizza's practically a balanced meal— you've got your bread and your meat and the tomato sauce counts as a vegetable, then there's cheese for dairy."

"In your own twisted logic, I'm sure that makes sense," she said. She stepped closer and placed one hand on his forearm.

He drew heart from that and lifted her hand, turned the palm up and kissed it right in the center. Her indrawn breath encouraged him more. "You've got me so twisted up, it's no wonder I can't think straight." He bent and placed his mouth just below her ear.

A soft hum sounded in her throat, and he traced the path to the spot, grazing kisses at intervals. When her head fell back, he slicked his tongue to the hollow and was rewarded by a soft gasp. He brought her body to his and captured her mouth, sliding his free hand into her hair to hold her in place. She went loose and pliant in his embrace.

She trembled, and Garrett had to pause to gather what little control he could manage. "You are so beautiful," he murmured. "So sweet."

She raked fingers into his hair and held him to her with a small cry. "Garrett, please…"

He stayed right where he was. She could urge all she wanted, but he was not sacrificing one sweet second to haste.

Half-crazed for her, he stumbled over his own feet and barely avoided crashing them both to the floor on his way back to the bedroom.

CHAPTER NINE

GRACE STRETCHED SENSUOUSLY as consciousness crept in on tiny cat feet. That's how she felt, feline and replete and… She rolled to her side, tucked one hand beneath her cheek and curled up, not ready to open her eyes because she hadn't felt this wonderful since—

Her eyes flew open as memory pounced.

There was a man in her bed…no, not her bed; she'd never seen this bed….

Garrett. It was Garrett, fast asleep beside her.

And neither had a stich on. She'd never slept that way, not even with Todd.

Todd. Grace waited for grief to set in, for inevitable guilt to follow. They did, but only a little. Only shadows of their former ability to render her weak and helpless.

Memories of what she and Garrett had done last night, however, possessed punch to spare.

Todd was gone. She'd loved him so much, but however unfair his loss, he would never be with her again except in memories of a life she had loved.

A life that was over. While she had no choice but to go on.

She was so very tired of being alone. She adored her children; she loved her work. If she'd thought to live out her life only as mother and businesswoman, last night had demonstrated vividly that both were fulfilling, yes, and important. But not enough.

Grace wanted more. She'd be dishonest to deny it. Maybe, just maybe, it wasn't wrong for her to live. To wish to be loved.

The man whose strong, muscled back faced her like a feast wasn't the one. He'd been clear on that. *Good thing I never wanted children.* However terrific he was with hers, he had only been playing with them. Being a playmate was easy; being a parent could be very, very hard. A lot of tough choices and always the knowledge that if push came to shove, their needs came first.

For a moment, Grace sagged under the disappointment that she couldn't magically find her other half, that however astonishing the hours she'd just shared with Garrett, he wasn't Prince Charming come to sweep her off her feet and solve all her problems.

Oh, grow up, Grace. She found a smile at the thought. One thing motherhood definitely did was make one a realist. Even if she hadn't been through widowhood and the scramble to get them back on sound footing after losing the breadwinner of their family, she would have already learned that wanting something to be true didn't make it so.

Garrett was not The One. Oh, he could be—she thought that was at least a possibility, given the surprises she continued to uncover within him. He was a good man, an honorable one, and he could be kind and caring and tender.

He could also scorch her socks off.

But he'd been clear from early on that family was not for him. The little she'd learned about his upbringing, it was no wonder he had severe doubts. He, better than most, understood that bearing offspring was light-years away from nurturing a child, from giving that child the solid foundation he deserved.

He'd deserved that, too, and her mother's heart grieved that he'd been denied it.

A treacherous part of her wanted to argue, to posit that Garrett had love to give, that he could be a good father if only he believed it, that she could make the difference, she and her children....

But if she cared about him, as she was beginning to realize she did, she would not burden him with any of that, now of all times. He was under intense pressure to perform, and crunch time was at hand. He had one race to prove himself, one race only, while the fate of many others rested in his hands.

So if she honestly cared about him, her choice was simple: either enjoy these few brief days with him with no expectations of a future beyond perhaps the occasional dinner…and maybe even more interludes of bliss like the one she'd just experienced.

Or walk away now.

Which might be the wiser decision, but she was so tired of always being wise. Didn't she, too, deserve a break? A small vacation from her life? Her children were in the best of hands and were accustomed to short absences like this. She would take care of her business here as Garrett would have to take care of his own.

But when they could steal the time together, she would see to it that they had fun.

Fun. What a concept. She was still mulling it over when Garrett stirred, rolled over.

Then he opened his eyes and simply watched, as though waiting to see what she was thinking.

You can do this. Not like it was a hardship, anyway, having a drop-dead gorgeous man within arm's reach.

So Grace slowly smiled, as memories of the night before hovered in the air between them.

Garrett's brown eyes melted to warm gold as he reached for her. "Come here, beautiful." His slow, tantalizing touch made her tingle all over again.

"Why don't you come get me?" Before she could think twice or he could react, she emerged from the bed, yanked the sheet away, wrapped it around her and took off.

And squealed like a teenager as Garrett leaped from the mattress and gave chase.

"YOU'RE GOING TO KILL ME, woman." Garrett had enjoyed his share of relationships, but he couldn't recall a woman making him wheeze...from laughing like a loon the whole time.

Somehow the hilarity put an edge of danger into the act, spinning them loose, making them silly and often on the edge of awkward. How could you be a dashing hero when you snorted out loud because the woman you were with was tickling you, for God's sake? Yet the lack of control was as energizing and seductive as it was scary. Didn't every man know his job was to be strong and skillful and dignified—at least, as dignified as sex could be?

Yet he didn't feel unmanned, he felt free. Accepted as someone real, something besides a poster boy, an image on a pedestal. A commodity to be traded upon for a few fleeting years until the limelight moved on.

And when Grace had paused to tenderly kiss the scar on his thigh from an ill-fated motorcycle ride, he'd experienced a staggering rush of emotion, a sense of benediction, a healing affection that contrasted sharply with the censure he'd received at the time.

"We should move," she said in that husky voice he'd become intimately acquainted with over the last several hours. "But the sun feels so good."

"It does." She was right, of course. They both had duties and obligations that would consume much of the day, but as they lay in the patch of sunlight on the floor in the living area of his motor home, Garrett experienced a surprising desire to wish the world away and just stay here with Grace.

"Mmm." She nuzzled her nose into his armpit.

Shocked, he tried to pull away, but she clung to him. "I need a shower."

He felt her smile against his skin. "This is going to sound totally perverted, but I like the smell of you all sweaty."

He grinned down at her. "That, Miss Grace, has to be a flat-out lie."

"I mean it." She rose and sat beside him, stretching and shaking her tousled curls.

She stole his breath, pale skin and fair hair gilded by the sun, arms extended, the curve of breast and waist and hip outlined in shadow. He laid a hand on her thigh. "Stay." It was as much of a plea—more than, really—as any he'd ever made to a woman in his life.

She let her arms fall, but her eyes were kind. "We both have appointments we can't miss." She smiled softly. "But I wish we could."

He rose to sitting beside her, touched her cheek. "Tonight, I mean. Don't go to your hotel."

Her conflict was visible. "Garrett, I—"

Just then, a cell phone rang. "Must be yours. Unless someone's changed my ringtone." Whatever it was sounded decidedly Disney.

"Millie's turn to choose this month. *Lady and the Tramp.*" Her look was apologetic. "I have to answer. It might be about the kids." She raced toward the purse she'd dropped on the sofa last night when they'd arrived. She frowned as she punched a button while struggling with the drooping sheet that was giving him enticing glimpses. "Hi, Ethan." She listened for a minute. "No, I'm fine. I don't need a ride to the track." She glanced at Garrett and bit her lip.

He only grinned.

She stuck her tongue out at him.

She shouldn't do that. It wouldn't take much to have him by her side, doing something far better with that tongue.

"No, really, it's not a problem. Um, I have to check on my supplies, then meet with the ESPN producer at five. What time is it?" Her brows flew upward. "Oh, lordy. No—no, I'm fine. I'll make it." She listened again. "Where are you parked?" At that, her eyes widened more, and she darted an alarmed glance at him, then pointed outside. "Uh, I'm not sure about dinner. What's your schedule?" More silence as she focused. "Okay, I'll call you after I finish with the producer, and we'll figure things out. Yes, I'll be careful." She rolled her eyes. "I love you, too."

Then she clicked off her phone and looked at him. "I have to shower and be out of here in forty-five minutes, and Ethan is parked about six spaces that way." She pointed.

"Piece of cake," he said, sauntering toward her.

"Stay there." She began backing up. "I don't have time for you, Garrett Clark. You may be experienced at sneaking around, but I'm not. I have to compose myself and take a shower and get dressed and—"

He moved in fast, lowered his shoulder and tossed her over it. "We'll shower together. Tight quarters, but it'll save time. Anyway, showering together is environmentally conscious. The only responsible thing to do, don't you agree?"

She was muttering into his back as he started the water, but she soon saw the wisdom of his argument.

"WOULD IT BE OKAY IF I LEFT my bag here until later?" she asked, adjusting the fitted jacket of her pale blue pantsuit while looking in the mirror. When Garrett didn't answer, she turned. "What?"

Caramel eyes studied her with the unholy gleam that never failed to send a spiky thrill through her. This time, however, something more serious tinted the edges. "I'd like you to stay, Grace, you know that."

"But Ethan would…"

"You're a grown woman. Do you need Ethan to tell you what to do?"

"Of course not."

"Then you're ashamed of being with me."

"It's not that. You're being intentionally dense. I risked one night because not a lot of people had arrived, but I have to do business with these people. NASCAR events have made my business grow, and there's the cookbook…. I have children to support, and I can't become an object of gossip."

She laid her hand on his arm to take any sting from her words. "We operate inside a very small circle, and eyes are everywhere on race weekends." Each word of logic lashed at the soft underbelly of their dreamy interlude, and she mourned that more than he could know. "Please understand, there's only me to take care of them. When Todd was killed so unexpectedly, we'd just bought our house, we had loans on both cars and he had only a small life insurance policy. I was mostly a stay-at-home mom who did catering jobs for extra money. I can't begin to tell you how terrified I was— still am, at times. It's only me," she repeated. "I'm all my children have."

Chagrin shadowed his face as he drew her into his arms. "I'm sorry. I didn't realize…I never thought about your situation that way. You're always so competent and in control. You make it look easy."

"Don't I wish." She sighed and allowed herself to nestle against him in both sorrow and relief. "I would love nothing better than to stay with you." She lifted her head. "Last night, this morning…I've never experienced anything like it."

"Never?" Delight, boyish and endearing, sparked.

After a hesitation, she nodded, responding to an inner hunger she sensed from him. Guilt over how the admission reflected on Todd layered over a wry acceptance of Garrett's far greater experience.

His hand lay warm against her cheek. "Me, either, Grace. I swear it." He lowered his head, and she fell still, for a careless instant foolishly wishing, however poor the odds, that there could be more to this than one night. One fling.

His lips brushed softly over hers, and she couldn't let him go just yet, couldn't end this respite. She rose to her toes and poured herself into the kiss with all the words she did not dare say.

It was a kiss of surpassing sweetness, flavored with the tart cherry of regret and the honey of longing, underlain by the dark chocolate notes of yet-unquenched passion.

She knew she should draw away, but she couldn't bring herself to. She was grateful when Garrett did, even as she yearned to grip him tightly and slip back into the reverie they'd shared.

"Will you let me come calling, Miss Grace? This weekend is packed for both of us, I know." No sign of teasing now. "But it would mean a lot to me to see you as often as possible. Even if that means sneaking around, if that's the only way you'll have it."

"Garrett, it's not that—" She sighed. "I wish this weren't so complicated."

"Since it's my bad reputation that's causing the problem, I can hardly take offense, now can I?" His words were easy, his tone relaxed. In his eyes, though, she could have sworn she spotted traces of hurt.

Remember the kids. However much she wanted to soothe him, to abandon herself to the sinfully delicious pleasure of his company, her children's welfare had to come first.

She snapped back to full reality. "I can't do this. I'm sorry, Garrett." With effort she pulled herself back to the Grace she had to be. "Honestly I am, but we shouldn't kid ourselves. It's better to stop here. I was wrong to mislead you, though I never meant to. I just can't see any way for this to work." She reached for her purse and bent to extend the handle of her carry-on.

His face closed down, his voice gone sharp. "Leave it here. You don't have to see me in order to get it later. My driver can bring it to you at your hotel."

Her impulse was to turn back to him, to try once more to explain.

But there was no way to make this right. They had no future, and she should never have spent the night with him. The explosive memories of it would only serve to torment her in the days and years to come.

"Thank you" was all she could think to say. As his steps

followed hers to the door, she halted. "You don't need to see me out."

"I don't know what the hell kind of man you think I am, but I am not making love to you all night and then simply shooing you out the door."

"But if we're seen—"

"We met early to talk about you catering an event. Will that satisfy your need to put me in my place?"

She heard the pain beneath the fury, and felt lower still for causing it. "Please, Garrett. Just let me go."

"Grace—" He muttered an oath. "Is this what you really want? Because it feels all wrong."

"It'll be easier. Please."

"You got it." He hastened to remove himself from her side, and she mourned the loss of his warmth, hating the new, miserable distance that was clearly best for them.

She left the motor home, stumbling on the last step. Wishing she could blame it on high heels and not tears.

From inside came the thud of a fist against a wall.

I'm sorry, Garrett. More than you can know.

She slipped on her sunglasses and forced her head high so that she could pull off the illusion that she'd had a business meeting, but every step away from him dragged pieces from her heart.

Only moments later came the last voice she wanted to hear right now. "Grace? Is that you?"

"Ethan." *Get it together.*

"What are you doing here inside the lot? I'm surprised you made it so quickly."

Never had she been more grateful for a pair of sunglasses. "You know me, always early. I have a little time before my meeting, and I wondered if you wanted to get a cup of coffee." *Say no. Please say no.*

"I should be in the garage, but I guess I could—"

She grabbed his arm and leaned into the strength of the man who'd been both brother and hero for most of her life.

"That's okay, really. I just—" She hugged his arm more tightly. "I'm glad to see you, even if only for a few minutes."

He looked down at her. "Are you all right?"

"Of course." She pasted on a smile and racked her brain for a distraction. "So tell me, does Sadie get to come to the big finale?" Ethan's daughter had come to live with him recently, and she had taken to racing like a duck to water. Mostly, Grace thought, because she loved being with her father.

He shook his head. "Think I could keep her away?" He grinned. "Cassie's feeling a lot better in her second trimester, so she's bringing Sadie down tomorrow. That way Sadie only misses one day of school."

"She's so bright she could probably miss a month and never notice."

"She is, isn't she?" Ethan beamed.

Grace found honest amusement at how gobsmacked her big brother was by the child he'd thought himself unable to raise after her mother died. Sadie's maternal grandparents had not wanted to let go of her, but Grace was very happy they finally had. Ethan would never have met his new wife, Cassie, if he hadn't needed a nanny, and he was long overdue for happiness.

"My kids will be devastated that Sadie got to come and they didn't. They adore her."

"Like Dad and Hope aren't spoiling them rotten even as we speak."

"I don't know what I'd do without Daddy's help. All of you have been wonderful."

He patted the hand tucked in his elbow. "There's nothing we wouldn't do for you, sis, you know that. Mom would haunt us if we didn't stick together."

She glanced up at him. "Any word from the detective?"

He halted, turmoil on his features. "I, uh, I didn't want to tell you yet."

"What?"

"Jared called me last night." He hesitated again.

"Go on, Ethan. Whatever it is."

"Mom was a nurse, Grace. The P.I. found records of her nursing license. In Tennessee." He paused. "Gina and Kent Grosso were born in Nashville."

"No. Oh, Ethan." She clutched at his arm.

"That's all, though. No one can say if she worked at that hospital or even in Nashville. The hospital is checking personnel records, but it was thirty years ago, so they may not be able to find anything."

"But she never told us she was a nurse."

"Why would she? Once she married Dad, she seemed perfectly happy to be a stay-at-home mom for all of us, don't you think? That was her past. It could be a coincidence. It proves nothing about what Susan claims." He clenched his jaw in that manner he had when he would brook no opposition.

"I want to believe that, but what if there turns out to be more? What if she did play a part in the kidnapping? I just keep thinking about Patsy and Dean and how they must feel. Consider about how you felt, hardly seeing Sadie. What if you'd lost her altogether?"

His muscles went rigid beneath her hand. "I know. I do. But Mom was so good to us. She married Dad and made life fun and gentle and sweet. Dad was so happy. I just can't believe it." His brows snapped together. "Don't tell me you do."

"No! Of course not." But she recalled what Garrett had said about how difficult this was for Dean and Patsy. His earnest offer to get her and Patsy together so she could be reassured that Patsy was not harboring ill feelings, just for Grace's peace of mind.

Oh, Garrett. For a second, she couldn't help remembering a thud on a motor home wall. The bliss of the night.

The hurt she'd put in his eyes. *It would mean a lot to me.* She gnawed at her lip.

"Grace? Did you hear me?"

"Sorry. I was—never mind. What did you say?"

He peered closely at her. "You seem distracted or something today. Is it due to more than Mom?"

How ashamed she was that her mother was not responsible for her current turmoil. That she was caught by an urge to turn back the way she'd come. "I, uh, I'm juggling a lot of balls, that's all. This is a busy weekend for you, too."

"Amen to that. Jared, as well. Garrett Clark is using one of his engines, so there's a lot at stake for Jared's business. Clark's got no wiggle room. Everything's on the line. I don't envy that team the pressure they're under."

It would mean a lot to me. However impossible a future was for them, she itched to take back what she'd said to him when they'd parted. All he'd asked for was the next few days. She would never forgive herself if she could have helped him out and hadn't. "Ethan, listen, I know you're busy. You go ahead. I just remembered a call I need to make." She scrambled to locate her phone in her purse.

"I can walk you over to the media center first."

"No, that's okay. It's a little quieter over here, and I should make this call before my meeting." She lifted to her toes and kissed his cheek.

"How about dinner?"

"I'm a crew chief's daughter. Are you seriously going to tell me you have the faintest notion right now what time you'll be done this evening?"

He grinned. "Got me. Okay, but call me later, all right? Maybe we can work it out to meet."

"Will do." She waited for him to get far enough away.

Then she punched in what she hoped was Garrett's cell number. When the recording of his slow, sexy drawl came on, a little flutter ran through her, however disappointed she was not able to reach him.

"Garrett, it's Grace. I, uh…I'm sorry. I'm out of practice at this. I never dated anyone but Todd and…" This was terrifying. She sucked in a deep breath and continued. "If you're still speaking to me, would you please call me as soon as you get the chance? I, uh, I'd like to claim my rain check. The one you didn't really give me, but I'm hoping you will." She paused, then raced ahead to beat the beep. "I'm really sorry. I got scared and—" The beep sounded. Could she have been more disjointed? Less poised? If only it were possible to retrieve a message...

She glanced at her watch, then picked up the pace so she wouldn't be late for her meeting.

CHAPTER TEN

GARRETT HAD TO LEAVE the garage area or risk saying something he'd regret. Everyone was tense—his sponsors were full of advice, the team members were getting on each other's nerves and Andrew had drawn within himself.

He loved his fans and usually couldn't get enough of the contact with them, but right now, if one more person told him what to watch out for or how to drive this race, he couldn't promise he wouldn't pop off at them.

Not that everyone didn't have plenty of reason to be nervous. He'd screwed up enough in his life, his maverick tendency sometimes costing him more than the benefits of his talent. He was good, yes, good enough to be the best. Even his competitors would admit that.

But he kept finding ways to sabotage himself. He'd wanted to go his own way, had a rogue streak a mile wide and a deep-seated need to indulge it. Women loved that in him, and he'd stood out from the crowd because many of his gambles had paid off.

Right now, though, when the chips were down and the stakes couldn't be higher, he wished he had some reliable groove he could slip into and know that if he just played his game, he was likely to win.

A gambler had to stay light on his feet, the kind of tap dancing that depended solely on his wits and his nerve…but luck could go his way or not.

He'd gambled with Grace and look how that had worked

out. The most astonishing night of his life, complete with a teasing sense that something he'd never dreamed could be his was nearly within reach. For the first time, he'd opened himself, become someone beyond Garrett the playboy.

Then Grace had called it quits before they'd really begun.

He knew better, didn't he? Love was a myth, and no one stayed. Anyway, Garrett Clark was just like his mother…great in the short run, lousy for the long term. Andrew had stuck with him, yes, but if Garrett cost him the team, how long would he be welcome in Andrew's life? How could he look his stepfather in the face, or any of the rest of them, for that matter?

He walked, but he wasn't sure where he was going. Not back to his motor home, not with all the memories lingering there. He could grab a bite, but he wasn't that hungry.

Maybe he should call someone. A woman, one who would help erase the taste of Grace, remind him that the world was full of women and he had his pick of them.

He should, most likely. But he didn't want to.

I just can't see any way for this to work. She was probably right, he knew that. But damn it, he didn't want her to be. He didn't like that she made him look at himself in a light that exposed the emptiness of who he was. He had toys galore, had fame, had women at his beck and call. Most men would think he had everything.

He was furious that all he could seem to want was Grace.

Forget her. Call someone who's good for a laugh and a good time. You've got to relax or you'll never win this race.

Angrily, he clicked on the phone he'd turned off in the garage so he wouldn't be rude by answering it when fans were waiting at the window to claim a few minutes of his time.

The tone for a voice mail sounded, and he pressed the key to retrieve it without bothering to see who the message was from. At this point, he'd welcome a conversation with the devil himself to distract him from his stormy thoughts.

"Garrett, it's Grace." He gripped the phone and clapped

a hand over his other ear to be sure he could hear. He listened all the way through, then punched the number to repeat and listened to her message again, a smile spreading on his face.

She was scared. How about that? Was it possible that she felt it, too, whatever this was between them?

I just can't see any way for this to work.

Don't bet on it, honey. The gambler in him would always rise to such a challenge. Grinning, he retrieved her number and hit the call button.

"Grace Winters," she said in that oh-so-professional tone that made him want to tousle her hair, to unbutton that severe jacket she probably thought provided protection.

"Where are you?"

Her indrawn breath was rewarding and seductive as hell. "I, uh, I'll be finished here in a few moments. May I call you back?" She sounded so prim he wanted to sink his teeth into her nape while he ran his hands all over her.

"Are you still at the media center? I'm headed your way."

"I'm not sure that's a good idea."

His delight dimmed. "Still don't want to be seen with me?"

"No! That's not—all right," she agreed, both irritated and trying not to be. Clearly, she was not alone. "I can meet you at the Chalet Village in about fifteen minutes, and we can discuss your project."

"Talking wasn't what I had in mind, Miss Grace," he purposely drawled, though he knew there was little more they could do in public. For now, at least.

Another sexy hitch of breath. "I'll see you later, Mr. Clark," she said in her best business tone, then severed the connection.

So how would he play this? How far could he push her to get what he wanted when he himself wasn't sure what that might be?

He was insane for complicating his life this week, when his career was on the line. But he'd spoken from the heart when he'd told her that it would mean a lot to him to spend as much of this weekend with her as possible.

It wasn't like him to look into the future, not where relationships were concerned, so why was he feeling the need to pin down more than right now with Grace?

"Garrett! Look, Sue, it's Garrett Clark. Can we get your autograph?"

He realized he'd stopped in one place too long, and he'd been spotted. "Sure thing." He smiled at the couple. "Where are you all from?"

"Alabama."

"Love that Talladega," he said, signing the hat and die-cast car and T-shirt they proffered. "One of my favorite tracks. See you all there in the spring?" He chatted with them for a couple of minutes and signed several more souvenirs for others. "Got a pretty lady waiting for me, so I'll have to say goodbye, folks."

The assembled group chuckled. "You're gonna win this race," the first man announced. "I can feel it."

"That's my thinking, too," he responded with a salute. "Thank you all for your support." He meant every word of it.

He picked up the pace and began to jog toward his meeting place, his heart lightened by the faith of his fans, yes, but even more by the knowledge that whatever that buttoned-up brain of Grace's was thinking, she'd taken the first step back toward him.

She was talking to one of the announcers outside the media center when she spotted him and visibly stiffened. To her credit, she cast him a smile, but he wondered how she would react, should he stroll over and join them.

He resolved not to take her discomfort personally and didn't press the issue. However increasingly intrigued by her he was, he didn't know where any of this would go, so it wasn't fair to put her under the microscope the television announcer could so easily bring to bear.

Instead he nodded toward the pedestrian tunnel and raised

his eyebrows in question. When she gratefully nodded back, he headed in that direction, wishing that he didn't know every fourth person inside the infield so that he and Grace didn't have to contend with unwanted attention. His motor home was the one place they could be alone, but it was situated where there was no chance of avoiding notice without the cover of night.

There was her hotel, the very one he'd tried to talk her out of. Getting there today wouldn't be a big issue, but beginning tomorrow, traffic would be a challenge all the way through Sunday.

Then a notion struck him. Two, in fact. He'd figure out Grace's schedule for the rest of the day and hope that her evening, like his, was fairly open. As the plan formed in his brain, he felt hope stir. The rest of the weekend would be crazy, but he would take however much time with her he could get.

Once he was through the tunnel, he found an observation spot and waited for her. Before she saw him, he lifted his phone and dialed her again. It was kind of a kick to see her dig for hers in her purse, to watch her expression when she didn't know he was nearby.

"Grace Winters."

"I have a solution."

"For what?"

"To preserve your reputation."

"Garrett, I'm not—don't worry about that."

"No, it's okay. It stung, but I've earned it." At her sound of protest he hurried on. "Anyway, forget that. Here's the deal. Look to your right."

She frowned a little as she scanned the area. When she spotted him, he'd swear he felt it. She began walking toward him.

"No, stop," he said.

"Why?"

"Because this is how we'll work this. We're going to have our chat, maybe say something naughty if we're lucky—"

"Garrett!"

Damn, but she was cute when she blushed. "Let me finish. We'll stay within sight, but no one knows who we're talking to. We can talk as long as we want. We'll have lunch together—I'm paying, by the way—but anybody who sees us will think we just happen to be in the same area."

"And how do you explain buying my lunch?"

"I didn't say it had to be a clandestine CIA exercise, you know. Just that we mostly keep some physical distance." He paused. "Because that's the only way we're gonna talk, babe. Otherwise, I am not man enough to keep my hands off you. Not after you blew the top of my head off last night."

"Garrett!" Her rosy cheeks were clearly visible now. She lowered her voice. "Is this the naughty part?"

"Oh, honey, I've barely started."

She looked both unnerved and inordinately pleased. "You are insane."

"Possibly. But it's a great idea, don't you agree?"

He watched her shoulders relax. "It's certainly different." But she was smiling.

"So…how did your meeting go?"

"Pretty terrific. I'm going to be on the prerace show."

"Wow, that's awesome."

"I know. So how has your morning been?"

"Don't ask. I'm on the lam from the garage."

"What? Why?" There was laughter in her voice, but it quickly sobered. "Are things bad? Is there anything I can do?"

"You're doing it. You're calming the driver down. And yes, bad is an understatement. The pressure's getting to everyone."

"You can handle it," she said with absolute certainty.

"Usually I'd say no question. Being a driver is all about handling pressure, and I'm no novice, but—"

"But what?" Her tone—and the look she gave him from where she stood, her move to approach him—made him believe she really wanted to know.

He normally never talked about nerves, convinced talking

only made them worse. Action was all that counted. Grace would listen without judgment, somehow he knew that. She would not offer advice. If he were going to confide in anyone, it would be her.

But she was dangerous, nonetheless, simply because she made him want to let go, and he couldn't risk unraveling, not now. His team was unnerved; he had to be the voice of confidence to pull them all through.

"But nothing. I'll be fine."

He saw disappointment blossom and hastened to change the topic. "So what should we have for lunch, hot dogs or hamburgers?"

Her shudder was visible, provoking a chuckle from him. "Oh, come on, Gourmet Girl. A certain amount of junk food is necessary for your health."

She was observing him closely, tempted, he would guess, to push the conversation back to the answer he'd dodged.

He was relieved when she decided to play along. "Oh, excuse me, Dr. Nutrition, did I miss your last book on healthy living?"

He grinned. "I was talking about mental health. Comfort food is good for the soul. You can't tell me you're in favor of ignoring the mind-body connection."

She sighed. "Why is it that most men eat like overgrown children?"

"Why is it," he mocked, "that women get so prissy about food?"

The light of battle flared in her eyes. "I'm not prissy."

"Oh, darlin'…I would so very much like to give you a chance to demonstrate that. Shall we adjourn to my bachelor pad?"

She rolled her eyes. "I think you'd better buy me a hot dog instead."

He clapped a hand to his chest. "You wound me, sugar. Still, never let it be said I spare any expense when it comes to seduction." With a courtier's bow, he indicated the stand nearby. "After you, madam."

"Why, thank you, kind sir."

"After which we'll discuss my idea for dinner."

Grace opened her mouth but didn't speak. Instead, she turned and led the way, the sway of her hips in those slim pants holding him in thrall.

She glanced back, brow lifted.

"Um, yeah, be right there." *Man, oh man.* Garrett shook off myriad fantasies and hastened to catch up.

CHAPTER ELEVEN

WEAR SOMETHING COMFORTABLE—that's all the clue Garrett would give her.

Grace paced her hotel room later in the afternoon and examined one of only two choices of outfits she had with her. She'd packed two options for the long pants required for any time spent in the garage area, but she couldn't afford to get her khakis dirty when she'd need them tomorrow. Saturday she would wear the slim black pants she wore when catering, and she always worried about hotel laundry and dry cleaning schedules.

That left a pair of comfortable jeans she'd tossed in for downtime with Ethan…okay, or with Garrett. Or the sundress she was currently wearing. It was November, but they were in Florida. She'd brought a cotton sweater, just in case…

Her room phone rang, not her cell. "Hello?"

"Ms. Winters, there's a gentleman named Stanley here for you. He says he's Mr. Clark's driver and that you're expecting him."

Mr. Clark's driver? Garrett, what are you doing? He hadn't said he was sending someone, but coming himself would be a risk. She should appreciate his discretion. She'd declared the terms, after all. It was just that after talking to him on the phone for two hours this afternoon while separated by at least several feet most of the time, she'd been looking forward to being with him—truly with him. "Of course," she answered. "I'll be right down."

He never did what she expected, she mused on the elevator

down, but he was certainly not boring. She'd never had a more fun phone call or one so…stimulating.

The man could make a nun recant. Have mercy, he was beyond hot, especially now that she'd known the incredible pleasure of being intimate with him.

But he was also sweet and fun and crazy in a good way. Her only frustration was that he didn't want to talk about the race, however much she sensed he needed the outlet. She couldn't and wouldn't push that, however, not at the risk of upsetting his balance. He was handling the intense pressure the way he knew best, and all she could do was be there for him. If he wanted to play, they'd play, and if he changed his mind and wanted to be serious, well, she'd be there.

She shouldn't be getting this involved, shouldn't care about him as she did. Logic, however, didn't seem to play any part in her reactions and, as she reminded herself regularly, she was a big girl. She'd been through worse than being dumped by Garrett Clark.

The elevator door opened, and she scanned the lobby for someone who looked like a Stanley.

"Ms. Winters." The man with the raspy voice who crossed the tiled expanse seemed to possess more physical grace than his girth would indicate. His face was shadowed by a Panama hat, and his eyes were hidden behind sunglasses. His Hawaiian shirt could make eyes bleed, and his pants bore an oil stain right above one knee. She felt bad for doing it, but she couldn't help also noticing a sizable wart on his left cheek. Altogether, if the desk hadn't contacted her ahead of time, she might have been heading for the hills, he looked so disreputable. But he had used her name, as well.

"Stop looking at me like that," he said in a very familiar voice. "The clerk's going to call the cops. Behave yourself."

"Garrett?" She gasped, then clapped one hand over her widening grin. "Is that really you?"

between them, eyes smoldering. "We're in public," he muttered, closing his lids. "Public, public, public," he chanted. Then they snapped open. He lifted her hand to his mouth and slowly drew one finger inside, suckling gently at it, eyes on her the whole time.

"Garrett…" Was that her voice, so low and breathy? Her head fell back as he drew in a second one, the warm, wet lapping of his tongue turning her molten.

The lowering rays of the sun bathed her back as hunger cascaded through her. She fought to remain standing when what her body wanted was to sink to the deck and drag him down with her.

Abruptly he let her go. "You're killing me, darlin'." He cleared his throat. "And my surprise will be ruined if I don't take my hands off you this second." He moved toward the wheel.

Still stunned by the sensations coursing through her body, Grace could only stare at his retreating back and muse that he looked equally amazing and hot from behind. So much so that she found herself drawn closer, hand reaching out, nails ready to rake over his skin as she flexed her fingers like a cat's claw.

What on earth had happened to the soccer mom? The responsible widow?

"Um, Garrett?"

He turned, and the blazing heat of his hunger called to hers. "What?"

"Would you—" Her voice was so hoarse. She tried again. "Could you please put on a shirt?"

A quick, slashing grin of sheer delight. "What's it worth to you?" He waggled his fingers for her to come near.

"I think I'm going to watch the ocean." With what little resolution she could muster, she turned away from him and gripped the rail.

"Oh, babe, you are priceless." He paused. "Coward." He laughed and started the engine.

Breathe, Grace. Breathe.

"Keep your voice down, woman. There are race fans all over this lobby." He took her elbow and ushered her to the front door.

She barely resisted laughing until they were outside. "You look ridiculous."

"You look ridiculously hot," he retorted. He tipped his sunglasses down, unveiling a bone-melting gaze. Then he waggled his eyebrows and stroked the—eww—big hair sticking out of his wart. "How about a kiss, hmm?"

She leaned away from him while extending a finger toward his face in horrified fascination. "Where on earth did you get that?"

He opened the door to a different minivan. "Get in and I'll tell you. People are looking funny at the gorgeous babe and the dirty old guy like I'm kidnapping you or something. Smile for the audience, honey."

She did him one better. She placed her hands on either side of his face, one touching the overly dramatic wart, and kissed him hard. "That better?"

"You are making it very hard to keep my hands to myself, babe. Have mercy on me and get in the van."

"Such a nice minivan, too. You're coming to like them, right?"

He got in the driver's seat with a sneer. "I like them as a disguise. No driver would be caught dead in one."

"Yet you've done so twice—three times if you count riding in mine."

"Go ahead and be smug, honey. You're at my mercy now."

And didn't she just feel a little inner shiver at the thought of it? Not that she'd tell him. "So where are we going?"

"That's for me to know and you to find out." He glanced over at her as they wove through traffic. "But I think you'll like it. I hope so, anyway."

"Will it unman you if I tell you you're sweet to care?"

He clapped a hand to his heart and beseeched the heavens. "Sweet. While I'm driving a minivan. The woman has it in for me."

Has it bad for you, is more like it. Grace reminded herself of her pledge to simply enjoy this time for the interlude it was, to keep in mind that she'd vowed she could handle whatever came. "So tell me where you got that god-awful wart," she said to keep things light.

His smile was proud. "I have several more just like it. A couple of cool fake scars, too."

"Any mustaches or beards?"

"Yeah." He twirled an imaginary one. "Want to see my magic box of disguises?"

"Is that like *want to see my etchings?* Been there, done that, you know." If only her heart felt as light as her tone.

"Well, just ouch, Miss Grace." He waggled his eyebrows at her. "But you ain't seen nothin' yet." His grin was ripe with delicious promise.

Grace's fingers itched to touch him. To be touched by him.

Instead, she clasped them together in her lap and looked at the road ahead.

A few minutes later, they pulled into a parking spot at a marina. Garrett opened his door and rounded the car to hers. "Are you okay on boats? I should have asked."

His flicker of uncertainty, coming from a man whose image was pure cockiness, was only the more endearing. "I haven't been on the ocean in one, but I'm game."

"This is actually a bay, Biscayne Bay. The waves are more than on a lake, of course, but the waters are pretty calm today. Will you come with me?" He extended a hand.

She took it happily. He helped her from the car, then placed one warm hand on the small of her back as he led her over to a sleek powerboat. He was the perfect gentleman as he helped her aboard.

A stocky man in his late forties or so emerged from the cabin. "Good evening."

"Grace Winters, this is the real Stanley, my hauler driver."

"Nice to meet you," she said. "You're much better-looking than your stunt double."

Stanley grinned. "I keep asking him to pick a different name when he's slapping on those warts." He crossed the deck toward where they'd boarded. "All gassed up and ready. Everything else is below," he said to Garrett. "Nice to meet you, ma'am."

Garrett slapped him on the shoulder. "Thanks, man. I owe you."

"Not after what you did," Stanley said, glancing back at Grace. "You two have a good time." He leaped to the dock and waved as he departed.

"What does he mean, after what you did, if I may ask?"

Garrett flushed and busied himself removing his disguise. "It was no big deal. He has a nephew with some health problems, and I knew someone who could help."

She wanted to press for details, but his discomfort was clea She doubted, however, based on Stanley's expression, tha had truly been no big deal. "Has he been driving for you lon

But just then, Garrett stripped off the Hawaiian shirt began unwinding the elastic bandages securing the pad beneath. The emergence of his bare chest made her fe she'd even asked a question.

Instead, she itched to touch, to taste his skin. To fall back into the glories of last night.

"Grace?"

"Hmm?" She jerked her gaze to his.

"If you keep looking at me like that, we'll never out of the marina."

"And that would be bad, why?" Could this be he Winters? She'd had a passionate and fulfilling love Todd, but ever since his death, the needs of her body pushed so far into the background she'd almost for had them. Now, the merest look from Garrett had d every last nerve ending.

"Oh, Grace, you drive me insane." He closed t

GARRETT CAUTIONED HIMSELF to stick to the plan, though he craved to ride out farther from shore and drop anchor, then strip Grace and himself and make love to her until darkness fell. Or until dawn came, maybe.

In a perfect world, they could have that, could forget all else.

Unfortunately, they lived in the real one. He had no idea if she'd even like his plan.

"Oh, look, a lighthouse! It's beautiful."

So far, so good. He continued heading for it, throttling back the engine as they neared the marina on the tiny key.

"Are we stopping here?"

"We are. Is that okay?"

"Oh, yes." Her face glowed. "I've never seen one up close."

Even better. He concentrated on docking, then tied off the boat and went below, retrieving jackets for both of them along with a picnic basket. The wind could get very cool, especially as sunset beckoned.

Her smile widened. "A picnic?"

"Yes, and before you start worrying, I didn't cook it."

She laughed. "I wasn't worried."

"Liar. Come on. We have a climb ahead." He put the basket on the dock and handed her one of the jackets, then leaped to the boards and turned to help her out of the boat.

"A climb?" Her gaze went to the lighthouse. "Up there?"

"Are you afraid of heights?" He should have asked first.

"Nope." She glanced up. "But I don't see anyone up there. It's okay?"

"For us, it is." Not that the arrangements hadn't been a challenge.

"One of the perks of fame that might make up for having to wear warts?"

He ducked his head. "I guess." He'd spent so little time with any woman who didn't consider his high profile his most attractive asset that he found himself almost wanting to apologize for it.

She slipped her hand into his and squeezed. "I personally think Groucho glasses are sort of hot," she teased.

And just like that, she smoothed everything out. Made him feel not like a freak but like a normal guy. He kept her hand where it was and bent to her. "I'll be sure to carry a pair with me at all times." He pressed a quick kiss to those smiling lips. "Come on. We'll miss the sunset if you keep dawdling."

"Oh, yeah? Watch this." Before he could react, she'd stepped around him and was six steps above him.

Windblown and laughing, they raced to the top.

"NOW THIS IS THE LIFE," she said, leaning back against the stone wall. "Gorgeous view, good wine—really good, by the way—relatively decent food..." At his look of dismay, she burst into laughter and leaned forward, kissing his cheek. "I'm kidding. You did good, Garrett. I'm impressed."

"So is this the part where you expect me to admit that Stanley bought all of it?"

"Would you?"

"Hell, no. I told him what to get. Even picked the wine especially with you in mind."

"A man of many talents. Oh, look!" She sat up so that the railing wouldn't obscure the staggering sunset spreading rose and gold over the water as the first few stars appeared overhead. She spread a hand over her chest. "Garrett, it's breathtaking."

When he didn't answer, she glanced over and found him studying her. "What?"

"That would describe you, Grace. You take my breath away." His reverent tone crept past every barrier she'd thought to erect against his charm. His bewildered expression said he was as out of his depth as she was.

We can't get serious rushed to her lips, but he was drawing her into his arms. As she prepared for a full assault on her already stimulated senses, he surprised her yet again and turned her back to his chest, wrapping his arms around her as the sunset played out its glory before them.

Oh, I am in so much trouble. But wisely she held her tongue and let herself live in this moment…this perfect moment that life had taught her must be lived in and wrung for every drop of joy, every second.

Because in another instant, everything could change. What you treasured could be lost forever.

So when Garrett pressed his warm lips to her nape and held her tightly as she shivered, Grace let him surround her, his warmth and humor and daring—all that made him utterly unique.

And she simply savored.

The man…the moment…the magic.

CHAPTER TWELVE

RACE DAY DAWNED BRIGHT and early, three days later.

Garrett rolled over in his bed, surprised that he'd slept, even as exhausted as he'd been the night before. Then he remembered the two-hour phone conversation he'd had with Grace and realized that though she wasn't in bed with him—as he'd wished for, angled for, using every ounce of charm he'd ever possessed—she'd calmed him, as usual, even while she was teasing him or challenging him…or simply just driving him slowly out of his mind with lust.

But she wouldn't stay with him. And he couldn't stay with her. His crew chief, shoot, his whole team, it turned out, was staying at the same hotel. Not that he'd have been bothered by being caught with her, but she was still insisting that this was a fling, no more. That once the season was over, their lives would go on as before.

He crossed his arms beneath his head and stared at the ceiling. She'd stolen his line. He was the one who came and played, then sent the ladies on their way. Not empty-handed and certainly with good memories, but Garrett had always subscribed to the belief that there were all sorts of lovely flowers out there for the picking. That life didn't have to be too serious. Up to now, the only thing he'd been dead serious about was driving.

Somehow Grace had changed that, he wasn't sure when. It might have been while she was standing on the lighthouse deck, hair whipping in the wind, face glowing with pleasure.

Or when she'd lain beneath him the one precious night she'd stayed with him, her sumptuous body relaxed and replete with pleasure.

Or possibly when she cooked for him in her kitchen, surrounded by her children, and opened up an unused place in his heart.

The sun's rays struck the bed and reminded him that today he could only afford to think about one thing: the race. Nothing else could matter. Today was for all the marbles, and he couldn't be distracted by thoughts of anything or anyone else.

He wouldn't even see Grace until afterward because she was scheduled for that stint on the prerace show, a golden opportunity to push her book and her own show to a huge television audience, a real feather in her cap.

But damned if he didn't wish she could be there to see him off before he climbed into the car. He'd never let a woman walk him to his car before because none of them had really mattered.

He'd have let Grace do it, though.

Shake it off, son. You've had some amazing days with her here, every second you could grab together. That should be enough. Fun's over.

It's showtime now.

Garrett shoved back the covers and rose, headed for the shower, but he paused for a second and glanced back at the sheets, remembering how they looked with Grace's golden hair tumbled over the pillow, her curvy body tucked beneath them.

Right next to him. Right where she belonged.

I'm gonna win that race today, Miss Grace, and the championship, too.

And then I do believe I'm coming after you.

GRACE SAT IN THE SWIVEL CHAIR as the television makeup artist worked on her.

"Your skin is gorgeous, hon. You're smart to protect it from the sun, a natural blonde like you." The woman was chatty, and normally Grace would enjoy visiting with her, but today, her stomach was in knots.

And not all because this appearance could make a big difference for her and her family.

She'd tried to call Garrett to wish him luck, but there was too much noise in the garage area, so she'd had to settle for texting him, not even vaguely satisfying.

She wanted to be with him, to look him in the eye and make sure he understood that she had total faith in him, that she was behind him all the way on this very crucial day.

Why had she insisted on not staying with him last night? What did it really matter who saw them together?

She glanced at her watch and calculated. She was due on the set in half an hour. Her segment would require her presence for another thirty minutes. "Who around here would have the race event schedule?" she asked the makeup artist.

"Lisa should," the woman responded.

"Where would I find her?" Grace rose from her chair.

"Wait—I'm not quite finished."

How could her makeup matter? Despite his outward demeanor, Grace was painfully aware of how worried Garrett was. She should be with him. He said she relaxed him.

"Please. Tell me where Lisa is. It's really important."

"I'd better find her for you." The woman stared at her. "You okay, hon?"

"No. Please, I need to know where they are in the schedule right now."

"Sure thing. Why don't you sit down while I go? You don't want to mess up your hair." The woman patted her arm. "It's okay to be nervous about TV."

Grace didn't try to explain. The woman left, but Grace was too agitated to sit down.

When the two women returned, Lisa let Grace scan the minute-by-minute schedule NASCAR had provided the network. Grateful for the hard card that allowed her full access, Grace calculated madly, figuring how much time it would take to rush through the crowd once she was done and where Garrett's pit stall was from the show's set. Her heart sank. It would be so close.

She looked at Lisa. "Is there any wiggle room in the schedule for my appearance? I know it's late to ask, but it's really important."

"The producer won't be happy."

"Can I speak to him? There's someone—I can't let him down. I'm so sorry."

"Him, huh?" Lisa studied her. "Want to tell me who we're talking about?"

Grace hesitated. If she did, she and Garrett would definitely be out in the open. He might not—who was she kidding? She was the one who kept slamming on the brakes and forcing him to maintain a public distance.

"Garrett Clark. I—he'd like me to see him off, but I, well, I told him we can't be seen together in public."

"Are you nuts, girl?" exclaimed the makeup artist. "He's the hottest driver in NASCAR. Why on earth would you want to hide him?"

"It's really complicated." She turned to Lisa. "This race is critical, and I should be there to wish him luck. Can you help me?"

"Can I tell the cameraman to look for you at his car?"

Grace steeled herself against the automatic instinct to say *no*. "If that's what it takes to get me down there in time."

"You got it." Lisa headed for the door, then paused and turned back. "Garrett Clark, hmm?" She fanned herself, then gave Grace a thumbs-up. "You go, girl."

Grace teetered between embarrassment and pride.

"Come on, hon," said the makeup artist gently. "Let's get you all dolled up for your man."

Grace's stomach jittered. "He's not my man."

"Well, hon, he sure ain't chopped liver."

Grace laughed and settled into her chair. For good or for ill, she'd taken the leap. "No, he most certainly is not." What he was, or what they could be to each other, they'd have to see. Maybe there was nothing beyond this day, but he was a good man in a tough situation, and she would be there for him.

"Please say you kiss and tell. Slapping on makeup gets boring."

Grace grinned and shook her head. "Sorry."

The woman sighed. "I was afraid you'd say that."

THE ATMOSPHERE WAS ELECTRIC. There hadn't been a championship race quite like this before, not with three drivers all within such close range of each other. Some years all a champion had to do was finish in the top half and be careful not to wreck, but this race would be very different. He, Murphy and Branch would all have to compete hard with each other—but not too hard or risk falling completely out of contention.

One wrong move, and his season could be over. Nothing less than winning it all would ensure FastMax's survival. Garrett had to be both aggressive in his pursuit of the win—something he enjoyed—and cautious to the extreme, not his strong suit.

Man, he would have liked to see Grace this morning. Just breathe her in for a second. Let that calm way of hers ease him through all this waiting.

He'd be fine once he strapped in. There his focus narrowed to one thing and one thing only: the race. His world became his cockpit and the voices of his crew chief and spotter. He was in the zone, and the outside world ceased to exist.

Just a few more minutes, he told himself as he walked toward his car and the teammates assembling for the opening ceremony. He walked past Kent Grosso, holding his wife, Tanya, close, and Garrett nodded while inside, an unfamiliar envy stirred. He'd always liked his freedom, had felt it critical to avoid entanglement and all the emotions that could affect his performance on the track.

He saw Sophia Grosso Murphy beside the car in front of his, smiling up into Justin Murphy's eyes. None of the three vying for the championship had qualified for the pole; Branch was fourth, Murphy was sixth and Garrett was seventh. They'd start close together and likely would be there all day, barring disaster.

As he accepted slaps on the back from his crew and gave them in return, he couldn't help scanning the crowd and wondering if Grace was there watching.

I'm proud of you, she'd texted. *I know you're going to win. I'll be thinking of you.*

He'd saved the text like some goofy junior high kid. He'd like to be able to look at it again. How sad was that?

You do that, Grace Winters. You think of me.

But damn, he wished she were here.

Then he saw Andrew approaching, expression steady but his posture stiff, and Garrett put on his game face.

"GREAT JOB, GRACE," said the prerace show host. "Terrific segment, and the food…well, wow is all I can think to say. You're leaving the rest with us, right?" He appeared to be settling in for a chat as the network switched to the team of announcers that would call the race.

"Oh, yes, it's all yours, you and the crew, of course." Grace tried not to feel desperate about the fact that the national anthem would be beginning any second, and she wouldn't make it.

"Dave, you'll have to pardon Grace," said Lisa, approaching them. "She's got a prior engagement."

"Oh, really? You're not watching the race? You could sit up here with us," he offered.

"You don't get it, Dave. She has a hot driver to meet before the race starts."

Oh, lordy. Now she was in for it. But she'd already received warning.

"Which driver?"

"That's for me to know and you to find out." Lisa grabbed Grace's elbow and escorted her out. "Just keep watching the cameras."

It would be all over the media the second she reached Garrett. For an instant, Grace lost her nerve, and her steps slowed.

Then she thought about the yearning she sometimes caught in Garrett's eyes. The pressure he was under to succeed, however much he presented the image that he hadn't a care in the world.

He'd let his walls down with her, and she knew that a hungering heart lay inside that gorgeous exterior.

She couldn't let him down. "Thanks, Lisa," she called.

"Oh, no, thank you, Grace. You just gave me my next raise."

Grace only waved. No more time for second-guessing. All she could do was run, and pray that she made it.

GARRETT WAS PRETTY SURE it wasn't appropriate to pray to win, so when the benediction finished, he only added his own plea that everyone stay safe and that he do his best work.

He and his team exchanged high fives, then he turned to get into his car.

And then, for a second, he thought he heard her.

He told himself not to look, that it was only his imagination, simply a trick of the mind that would distract him. Now was the time to home in on the race and nothing else.

But he heard her again. "Garrett, wait!"

He turned, and there she was, dodging through a sea of uniforms and photographers, blonde hair flying behind her as she ran flat-out toward him.

Inside him, the sun rose and everything that was cold and scared warmed up. He smiled and held out his arms, and she ran right into them.

"I'm sorry, I tried to get here earlier, but—" She was gasping from her race. "I should have been here all along."

He laughed and twirled her in a circle. "Doesn't matter. I am so glad you're here now."

Her arms squeezed tightly around his neck as she clung to him. He wanted to stay like this forever, in this bubble that was only the two of them. "God, Grace, thank you. I needed this. I've been wishing for you." He buried his face in her neck.

"Um, Garrett," said his jackman from the side. "Everyone else is in their cars."

The bubble abruptly burst, and Garrett looked behind Grace to see dozens of cameras pointed in their direction. Oh, boy. "Babe, you do know that a few people are now aware that you're here with me, right?"

She drew back with laughter in her eyes. "Like a few million, maybe? I, uh, it's sort of my fault. I had to explain why I had to leave the studio early."

He was stunned. "You did this, knowing…? Are you sure?"

"I'm sure that people don't want to wait for us to have this discussion." She pressed a quick hard kiss to his lips. "Go win that championship. I know you can." She started to back away.

He grabbed her around the waist and pulled her right back. Laid a kiss on her that had his ears ringing. "Don't you go anywhere, hear me? I want you with me in Victory Lane."

Then he realized that the noise wasn't his ears but the crowd. He glanced up to see himself and Grace on the big screen above the scoring tower.

Her gaze followed his. She blushed furiously, but she hugged him once more. "Good luck. And be safe."

"I'm not going anywhere until you promise." Fortunately, the NASCAR official standing nearby was smiling, but he knew that couldn't last. The PR might be good for the sport, but the clock was ticking.

"I'm not going anywhere," she murmured in his ear. "See you in Victory Lane."

Reluctantly he let her go, then turned and waved to the crowd. Cheers rang out, along with laughter.

He was going to win, he knew it now. One last glance

back at her for good luck, then he climbed inside and put on his helmet.

"You are so gone," said Robbie into his headset.

"The Sanford spotter relayed a message from Ethan Hunt," said his spotter. "Says he'll personally kick your ass if you hurt her."

"I figured," responded Garrett, but he couldn't stop grinning.

"But then he said to wish you luck."

"I just got all the luck I need, but tell him thanks. Oh, and that I can take him. No, on second thought, better not."

"All right, children. You've provided the fans with scanners with enough entertainment for one day. We've got a race to win," growled Robbie.

Garrett allowed himself one more grin as he waved out the window to the cameras trained on him. Then the window net was sealed beside him.

"Fire it up," said Robbie in response to the Grand Marshal's call to start engines.

Garrett hit the switch. Very soon, the cars began rolling onto the track.

Showtime.

CHAPTER THIRTEEN

THE ROOKIE ON THE BOTTOM didn't have the experience to know he'd picked the worst possible moment to try to pass. Nineteen laps from the end of this race that meant everything for Garrett's future, his time sense throttled down, as it often did in a crisis, to a slow-motion camera. He saw the wiggle in the rookie's fender before his spotter could say a word, but just then, Will Branch decided to pass Garrett on the high side, and Garrett was trapped between a wicked loose car and a good driver who couldn't see the problem looming.

"Four sixty-seven on your bumper, your door. Five seventy-three on the bottom is loose—"

Garrett used split-second timing to let Branch get by while steering away from the rookie. Despite human instinct to slow down, he knew that would be the end of the race for himself and everyone behind him if he did, so he remained steady on the throttle and threaded his way forward, following Branch—

The tap on his left rear bumper sent him spinning.

His spotter was talking in his ear, but he was on autopilot, relying on honed reflexes and instincts, using every ounce of strength and wit as he fought not to hit the outside wall—

"Caution's out, caution's out—damn, Garrett, that was close," exulted his spotter. "You are the man!"

He didn't care about praise; all he cared about was the damage, both to his car and to his track position. "How far back am I from Murphy and Branch? How does the car look?" he asked as he started forward again from where he'd landed in the grass.

"Can't tell for sure from here," said Robbie. "How does it feel?"

Garrett was focusing everything on sensing his car's condition, not the sinking feeling in his gut. "Maybe a little left rear tire rub...I'm not detecting anything else. Robbie—what the hell did Carshalton think he was doing?"

"He's a rookie, Garrett," said his spotter, Jamie. "But you're not out of this. You're in twelfth, Branch is sixth, Murphy is second. You're two point three seconds behind him."

"Bring it on in when pit road opens," Robbie said. "We'll get you fixed up. You can do this, Garrett. Just got to work your way back up."

"How many laps left?"

"Sixteen, probably, by the time we go green again."

Garrett closed his eyes for a second and watched his dreams and his team's future slipping away.

"You just have to be patient," reminded Robbie.

Garrett could hear no stress in Robbie's voice but every single team member had to be feeling it. Getting down wouldn't help any of them. He forced a grin into his voice. "Best news I've heard all day, bein's that I'm so good at that."

Jamie snickered. Even Robbie chuckled a little.

Andrew came on the radio. "I believe in you, son. You're going to win this."

For a second, Garrett couldn't speak. "You better believe it. Okay, guys, get me back on the track as fast as you can, and let's see if there's still a rabbit in the top hat. Me, I've got a taste for champagne, how about you guys?"

In his headset, he heard other voices as the team keyed their mics to answer.

"Pit road open, come on in," said Jamie.

Thirteen point five seconds, including yanking out the left

rear fender. "You guys rock!" Garrett exulted as he hit the track two spots higher, in tenth. "Where are Branch and Murphy?"

"Murphy's still second. Branch lost one and is seventh."

"Piece of cake," Garrett responded, though it was anything but.

"Coming to the green," Jamie said, one lap later. "Fifteen laps to go.

Garrett bent to the task of pulling off a miracle.

"FOLKS, THIS IS UNBELIEVABLE," said the radio announcer into Grace's headset. "Before that last caution, Garrett Clark looked to be done in this run for the championship, but he has steadily worked his way up through the pack, showing patience this gifted but impulsive driver has often lacked in the past. With two laps to go, he's in second place but can't quite close on Justin Murphy."

Grace listened, hands clasped in prayer while staring at the big screen. She'd given up on listening to Garrett and his team, superstitious that somehow her tension would bleed through the airwaves and jinx him. She wanted badly to close her eyes, to take off her headset and wink away to somewhere that her stomach wasn't in knots for him, where she didn't feel so helpless.

"Last lap, folks, and Clark is right behind Murphy, trying for the high line he prefers, but Murphy has him blocked. He's running out of time—whoa, there he goes, sliding down for the pass…. Now he's in front, folks!"

"Uh-oh, his car is drifting up," the color commentator interjected. "He's going to hit the outside wall—holy smokes, will you look at him?"

"Only yards to go, and—oh no!" The announcer broke off.

Grace's heart pounded in terror. Prepared for the worst, she couldn't register at first what she saw.

"Unbelievable!" cried the announcer as the crowd roared even louder than the screaming engines. "One driver in a hundred could pull this off, but somehow he's managed to hold on, while Murphy has ducked down—Murphy's a little loose and Clark—they're neck and neck coming to the checker—"

Grace felt faint. She stared at the jumbo screen, everything in her focused on those two cars.

"Do you believe this? Clark did it—won the race by maybe six inches—folks, we've got a new champion, Garrett Clark!"

"That is the driving job of that boy's life," intoned the color commentator.

Grace's hands were shaking as she tried to switch to Garrett's channel.

All she could hear was shouting and cheering.

"You did it, you crazy sonofagun, you did it!"

"You are the man!"

Then at last, she heard him. "This is for you, Dad. You never gave up on me."

"Son…I don't know what to say," Andrew responded. "But I have to sit down."

They all laughed. Then Garrett spoke again. "Where's Grace? Put her on, would you?"

"Uh…she's not here, Garrett. She, uh—"

Grace ran madly for the war wagon. Robbie spotted her and removed his headset and handed it to her.

"I'm here, Garrett. I just…oh, I am so proud of you! Congratulations!"

"You'll be in Victory Lane, right? Just like you promised?"

"I shouldn't—this is for all of you, not me. I'm not a part of it."

"Oh, yes, you are, babe. Bobby, you escort her over there."

"You gonna do your burnout or you gonna yammer all day, Garrett?" asked Jamie.

GRACE WATCHED GARRETT'S jubilant burnout on the track while his team went absolutely nuts, cheering and slapping high fives and doing chest bumps.

Her hands were still glued together in front of her mouth. She couldn't seem to stop shaking from that daring move he'd executed just short of the finish line.

He'd bet all the marbles. He always would. He was larger than life, vital and magnetic and fearless in the clutch moment.

He took her breath away.

And scared her to death. She was a mother with three tender souls in her charge. She had to be careful every second. What had she been thinking? How could she ever have believed whatever this was between them could work? She'd known, deep in her gut, that the attraction between them was not the stuff of everyday life. Being with Garrett Clark was like touching a live wire with your bare hands.

"You coming, Ms. Winters?"

She jolted. A fresh-faced boy clad in a FastMax uniform stood before her. "What?"

"I'm Bobby. He's on his way to Victory Lane. We have to hurry."

She'd promised she'd be there, but how was that fair, to be seen so publicly with him again when they must inevitably part ways?

"I don't know," she replied. "Maybe I'd better not. This is your team's day."

"Ma'am," he said and made her feel about eighty, "he said he wanted you there, you know that." A flush rose up his neck. "I mean, surely after that kiss and all before the race…you don't want to bring him down right now, do you?" The young man's eyes shone. "He pulled off a miracle. I'm just proud to be able to say I wear the FastMax uniform. Damn—er, dang, but I've never seen anyone drive like that. I'll be telling my grandchildren about this one day."

His eagerness to be with his team was transparent, but he was clearly waiting for her. "You go ahead."

"Can't do that, ma'am. Mr. Clark himself asked me to

escort you through the crowd. It's crazy over there, everybody so excited. That was the finish of a lifetime, I do swear."

Grace was torn. Was it fair to celebrate with Garrett when she knew she would have to backtrack on the implied promises she'd made? She'd been caught up in the emotions of this race, this season…this amazing man who turned her inside out. But she had to stop it now. Wake up to reality.

But as she looked at this eager boy in front of her, she knew he was also right. The Garrett she'd come to know wasn't a playboy with no real feelings—he had a heart, and a good one, and his life had not been charmed.

This was Garrett's moment of glory, a high like no other in a driver's career. If she cared about him—which she did, however unsuited they were—how could she do anything to tarnish the joy he was experiencing? He'd laid everything on the line to win. And she'd assured herself she was strong enough to handle the aftermath of this fling with him.

She didn't feel so strong right this minute, but she didn't like breaking promises, either. "Well, what are we waiting for?" With effort she locked away everything but honest jubilation and pride at what he'd accomplished and focused on Garrett and what he deserved this night.

She'd slip away as soon as possible and head home to her real life. Garrett would be tied up for days with the PR whirlwind of a champion's victory tour. He'd be too busy to take a breath, much less miss her.

"This way, ma'am."

"One favor, please."

"Sure thing."

"Don't call me ma'am. Save that for your mother or your ninety-year-old auntie."

He grinned and tugged at the bill of his cap. "Yes, ma—um, yes, Ms. Winters."

"You can call me Grace."

"Okeydoke. Can you run fast, Grace? 'Cause we're gonna be late if we don't get a move on."

"Lead the way." She'd keep up if it killed her.

It nearly did, but when they got there, Garrett was already out of the car and in front of the cameras, sweaty and so beautiful, using that trademark charm to its fullest advantage as he was peppered with questions from a phalanx of reporters.

But his eyes flicked around the area often.

When he spotted her, his whole frame relaxed and a smile bloomed.

She felt it like a caress, and her heart hurt, but she gave him a big smile back.

Reporters turned to see what he was looking at, and she faltered, shaking her head at Garrett. *I'll wait,* she mouthed.

But it was too late. He was already plowing through the throng to get to her. She was only partially aware of the silence that fell, then the buzz that arose as people noted his intent expression.

Then he reached her and swept her up in his arms. "You came," he said in her ear.

"I said I would." *Traitor.* Then she pulled back. "You were amazing. That was a finish for the ages."

His trademark cocky grin flashed. "It was, wasn't it? So do I get another kiss for it?"

"Do you actually need any more media scrutiny?"

"Hell, live large, Grace." Then he kissed her, long and lavishly.

Since it would be the last one, she was selfish enough to indulge herself in it. She shamelessly savored every second, cheers ringing in her ears.

They drew apart laughing. "I'm so glad you're here," he said.

"Me, too." And she honestly was. If only… But this was not a moment for *if onlys*. She shoved gently at his shoulder. "I think you have a few more important things to do than kiss me."

"Never." He grasped her hand and pulled her along with him, headed toward the stage and his team.

"Garrett, I shouldn't—"

The grin he cast back at her was tinged with enough of the vulnerability she'd seen before that she gave up trying to hold herself apart.

Tonight was for celebrating.

Tomorrow was soon enough to mourn.

"I CANNOT WAIT TO GET you alone." Garrett practically had to shout in her ear to be heard, even as the celebration on the champion's stage was breaking up. They were both drenched with champagne and she fruitlessly tried to dry it with a sponsor towel someone had handed her.

"You have to go to the media center first, though, right?"

"Yeah." He sighed.

"You love it, you know you do. If you don't wring every last drop from this experience, you're crazy."

"Crazy about you," he replied. "Walk with me, okay?"

Her smile was almost too bright. "I'm so proud of you. And look at Andrew. I swear he's dropped ten years off his age."

What she said was true. The tension that had dogged his stepdad for months had drained away. "He's done so much for me. I owe him."

"He loves you, Garrett. Surely you see that."

"Doesn't matter. I still owe him. He took me in when my mother couldn't be bothered. I'm not his blood, but he treats me like I am." He winced. "Like the butt-chewing he gave me for what he calls that last stunt on the track. Other people are calling it a brilliant move."

"It was brilliant, but a lesser driver could never have managed."

"Yeah." He'd had no doubts, though. Winning was all that mattered, and it had been his only option. "Glad it worked out."

She halted. Placed her hands on his face. "I'm glad you weren't hurt when you got spun out. I was scared to death."

"I'm sorry. I didn't have time to be scared myself. You can't second-guess in a situation like that. You just have to drive the wheels off and trust your spotter and your skills."

"Garrett…" Those blue eyes were troubled.

"What is it? Are you okay?" She'd seemed a little off all evening. "Is something wrong?"

Like clicking to a new channel, her face cleared instantly. "No, of course not." But she dropped her hands and stepped back. "I just don't want you to be late, that's all. We've gotten enough attention for one day."

The woman who'd dared to run to him in front of millions, who'd cast off her usual caution, was nowhere in sight. "Are you having second thoughts, Grace?" In the pit of his stomach, he felt them, and he cursed that he couldn't simply whisk her away right now and lock the world out so that he could say what was in his heart and seal the bond between them.

She wouldn't look at him. "I'm just not used to all this attention."

"You, with the television show and the book about to come out? Get real."

"That's different. That's business. My personal life is something else."

"Are you still ashamed of being seen with me?" A sour taste rose in his throat.

"No." Her eyes locked fiercely on his. "I most certainly am not. I'm proud to be with you, it's just—" She shook her head. Gave a small laugh. "Look at me. It's been a really emotional day. First I was afraid that I wouldn't get there in time before the race, then I'm making a spectacle of myself before millions, then I'm watching you run the race of your life against impossible odds…you take my breath away, Garrett." Her gaze on him was warm and proud, if filled with nerves. "I don't have any practice. I'm mostly just a mom who likes to cook."

"You cook like an angel, and you're one hell of a mom." He pulled her into his body. "And you dazzle me, Miss Grace." He was about to kiss her when he heard his name shouted by his PR rep, Sunny Palmer.

"Duty calls," he sighed. "Will you be with me tonight? It won't be a complete celebration for me until we're together. Alone," he added.

"Don't you still have a team party to attend?"

"But you'll come with me, and we can sneak out early."

She rolled her eyes. "You're the star of the show. I highly doubt that."

Sunny hollered again and started toward them. "In a minute, I swear," he called back.

He returned his gaze to the woman in his arms. "Please, Grace. Give me this night." He put his heart into the plea. "You're the reason it all worked out."

Her eyes widened, and she gave a shy, pleased laugh. "I'm pretty sure my part was too tiny to be counted." Then she rose to her toes and kissed him. "But yes, I'll be waiting. Now go, before the natives get restless." Despite her words, she clung to him for a second.

He poured himself into another kiss. *I love you,* he wanted to say, but he didn't want the first time to be when he had to leave her, so he refrained. "It's going to be a night to remember, sweetheart."

She touched his cheek and smiled. He wished he had time to be sure the shadows were all gone, whatever their origin, but right then, his rep reached them.

"You may be the champion, but you still don't want to be late. Let's beat feet, hotshot," the woman said.

"I get no respect," he muttered, and cast one last look at Grace.

Wishing he could keep her beside him, so he'd be sure she wouldn't vanish.

CHAPTER FOURTEEN

GRACE TURNED FROM the media center, walking slowly, head down as she tried to figure her next step. He might be in there a long time; this was the end of the season, after all, and his finish had been one of the most exciting in years. It wasn't all that often that the same driver won the final race and the championship, as well. There were ample angles for stories, and a pool of reporters from all over the world waiting to lap up the details.

"Grace?"

She looked up to see her brothers, both of them. "What are you doing here? I thought you'd be wheels up by now."

They exchanged glances. Finally, Ethan spoke. "We, uh, wondered if you'd like to fly back with us. I'm holding our plane."

At the moment, nothing sounded better than hugging her children and crawling into her own bed. She'd canceled her ticket for the flight home tonight after Garrett had asked her yesterday to fly back with him, whether immediately after the race in case of a loss, or tomorrow because he'd won. She'd cleared it with her dad first and made sure her children were okay about it. Only Bella had complained, and that was because she thought she should come down there to be part of the hoopla.

But Grace had promised Garrett the night, and selfishly, she wanted one more with him herself. "I can't. I—I told Garrett I'd…" She cleared her throat and straightened to an almost-military posture. "I'm staying with him tonight."

Their pained expressions were nearly identical. In other circumstances, she'd laugh.

"Grace," Jared began. "Have you thought this through?"

"I've done little else."

"I don't know what Clark's appeal is—" Ethan winced. "Aside from the obvious, but you have children to think of."

That did it. "Don't you lecture me about children, Ethan Hunt, when you left your own child to be raised by someone else for ten years. And you—" She turned to Jared. "I am a grown woman. Now I grant you that this is out of character for me, but don't I deserve a little fun for a change? I adore my children and I love my work, but both of those are very demanding. Do I not have a right to some time for me when I'm not hurting anyone else?"

Ethan's expression was stormy, but Jared spoke first. "Of course you do. We've all encouraged you to go out, to date, just not…c'mon, Grace, Garrett Clark? He's a player. Everyone knows that, and there you were on the monster screen for the whole world to see."

"Don't say another word." It was hard to argue with their doubts when she had plenty of her own, but her turmoil was all she could deal with right now. "Look, I'm doing the best I can. Anyway, you don't really know Garrett the way I do. He's a good man. Surely the two of you have been in this business long enough to know there's a difference between a driver's image and the man beneath. He's been with a lot of women, yes—"

"And you've been with exactly one man," Ethan pointed out.

"So I'm too stupid, too naive to know when I'm being played—is that what you're thinking?"

"You're not stupid, Grace. Don't be ridiculous."

"But I am too naive?" Their expressions said it all. "I happen to disagree with you, but you know what? Even if you're right, it's my life, and my heart, and if I make a mistake, then I'm the one who pays, not you."

"Calm down," Ethan said. "You're getting too worked up."

"Well, what if I want to get worked up? What if I want to have a—an affair, a wild and crazy one? What business is it of yours?"

"We love you, sis, that's all," Jared responded.

That took the steam out of her. The tirade that had erupted from her confusion evaporated in the face of their love. "And I love you, even if you're both overbearing and nosy." She sniffed and walked into their arms. "I'm sorry. I know it looks crazy, and maybe it is." She relished the hugs each offered. "But he needs me. And it's only one night, all right? I already know it can't be more. We're too different." She brushed at her eyes. "He is a good man, though. If you knew him like I do, you'd realize that he'd never do anything to hurt me. I'm the one who's about to hurt him, and I feel like the lowest form of life about it. Let us just have this time, okay? He's on top of the world right now, and I don't want to ruin that, so I'm staying." She took a hand from each of them and squeezed. "You've always been good to me—at least when you weren't being a pain." She smiled at them. "I adore you both. And I want this night with Garrett before I have to start saying goodbye."

Ethan drew her into his broad chest, and for a second, she wanted to stay there where it was so safe. "If you change your mind, I'll come back to get you. Just say the word."

She drew back and kissed his cheek. "Thank you. Give my love to Cassie and Sadie." She turned to Jared and hugged him, too. "Go home to Evie and be grateful that you have her." Then she stepped away. "I'll be home by tomorrow afternoon. I'll fix dinner for all of us one night next week, all right?"

With obvious reluctance, her brothers left her.

Grace headed for the washroom to repair the damage before she returned to wait for Garrett.

THE TEAM PARTY WAS RAUCOUS, the atmosphere jubilant and electric. Grace indulged in more champagne than she normally would, a free woman for this one night.

Garrett was in his element, trading war stories about the season, slapping backs and exchanging chest bumps and hugs with various members of his team, toasting Andrew with a speech of such emotion that hers were not the only damp eyes in the room.

She was surprised at how many other drivers or team owners had stopped by to extend their congratulations instead of leaving town immediately. Her impression of Andrew Clark was of a quiet man who took life very seriously, but she knew from Garrett that within him burned a strong competitive streak, honed by years of standing in the shadow of the legendary Grosso family into which his sister Patsy had married.

Yet during Garrett's toast, Grace spotted Patsy and Dean Grosso, their features expressing only pride and happiness for Andrew, despite the fact that Garrett had just beaten their own son-in-law, Justin Murphy.

Patsy was scanning the room, and when her gaze landed on Grace, she went very still. For a moment, Grace could almost feel Patsy's eyes on her, as if some kind of current flowed between them. Suddenly Patsy's face began to crumple, and Grace knew it had to be her mother's deed that was at fault. She didn't know if she should go to Patsy or get out of her sight. Dean spoke into Patsy's ear, and Patsy pressed her lips together, then lifted her glass of champagne toward Grace.

Grace lifted hers in answer, hoping the gesture meant no hard feelings, and was relieved when Patsy smiled, however wobbly. Then someone shifted in front of Grace, and she lost sight of them.

As she stood puzzling over the exchange, Garrett appeared beside her. "Ready to make our escape?"

She turned in surprise. "Garrett, you can't leave yet. The party's still going full throttle. Your team will miss you."

"I miss you more." He nuzzled behind her ear. "My team won't care, as long as the bar stays open. And I want my reward for winning."

"The trophy's right over there."

"You, Grace. You're the real prize."

His hands were drifting where others couldn't see and driving her slowly out of her mind. Her mind was a mess because she wanted what she couldn't have, and she was so afraid of how much hurt lay ahead, but she couldn't figure how they could—

"I'm not doing this right if that brain is still firing on all cylinders." Garrett turned her to him, his eyes tiger-gold the way they got when desire rode him hard. "Come on, sweetheart. Tonight, I'm going to rock your world." His grin was full of mischief, but she could see beyond the charming byplay. She knew how seldom he let down the guard of his charisma and revealed what was in his heart.

It was a privilege that he would let her see him in his moments of doubt or need, and Grace did not have it in her to deny him now.

So she consigned her doubts and fears to a remote corner of her mind and focused only on this man and this amazing night when he'd performed a feat that would be remembered for a very long time. She set her glass down on the nearest surface and slid her arms around his neck, brushing her body against his. "Showing is always better than telling," she murmured, and laughed as she felt his body's powerful response. "Do your worst, Mr. Champion."

"Oh, no, Miss Grace. I intend to do my very, very best... all...night...long." He looped one strong arm around her waist and quickly wove a path through the crowd. Outside in the hall, he punched in Stanley's number on speed dial and told him where to meet them, never letting go of her once.

Stanley, as always, was on top of his game. In much less time than she'd have expected, they were whisked to her hotel.

She turned to him in surprise.

"I thought you might prefer this to being at the track. We'll have more privacy, and Stanley has to pack up the motor home and drive out first thing. He'll bring my bag and leave it downstairs. A car will be here in the morning to get us to the airport." He grimaced. "Then we'll drop you in Charlotte, but I have to go on to New York. I have a feeling I don't really want to know the exact schedule, but my rep has already warned me I won't have time to take a breath for the next week."

"It'll be exciting, though—late-night talk shows, daytime talk shows. Being wined and dined all over Manhattan."

His expression was part boyish delight and part reluctance. "It is, and it's not like I haven't worked for years to get there," he admitted, "but you know what I'm really looking forward to?"

She shook her head.

"Coming back to Charlotte and maybe talking my way into dinner at your house."

Oh, how she wanted that, too, however wrong it might be to delay the inevitable parting. "Even if that means dressing dolls with Millie and Bella or playing soccer with eight-year-olds?"

"Even if. *Especially* if, I'm starting to think. Grace—"

Stanley stopped the car in front of her hotel. "Here we are."

Garrett didn't finish what he'd been about to say, and she wasn't sure if she wanted to hear it or not. "Thank you, Stanley. It was wonderful to meet you."

"Oh, I bet I'll be seeing you around, Ms. Winters." Stanley's head inclined toward Garrett, who was standing outside holding the door. "By the look on his face, I'm counting on it."

"Please call me Grace." She didn't address his conviction, but at the edge of the seat, she paused. "Take good care of him, Stanley. Please." Then she stepped out of the car and into Garrett's waiting arms.

The trip up in the elevator hummed with all neither was saying. When they passed her floor, she looked at him.

Garrett waggled his eyebrows. "A few more surprises." At the top floor, he led her out and down a hallway to an impressive double door. When he opened it, she halted in astonishment.

There was a fairyland waiting for them, a lover's bower. A stunning array of flowers adorned every surface, and rose petals were scattered across the enormous bed. Beyond it, the drapes were open to a startling view of the Miami sky. The lighting was low and seductive. Sultry blues played softly in the background.

"Garrett…" She blinked her eyes once, then again. "How on earth…?"

He brought her hand to his lips. "I wasn't sure we'd get to use this, but I made the arrangements, anyway."

"If you hadn't won?"

"This has nothing to do with winning a race, Grace. This is only about you and me. I was determined to be here, either way." He opened her palm and pressed his mouth there, too. "You deserve some magic, and I want to give it to you."

"You already have, Garrett, but this…" She turned back to stare at it. "This is like a dream. I've never—" She shook her head. "This only happens in novels."

Slowly he reeled her in, tender kisses leading to long, heated ones. "We're writing our own story, and I want it to have a happy ending."

"I can't think," she said.

"Don't," he replied, his hands roaming. "Just feel tonight, Grace."

Her head fell back and she gave up on logic and what was practical and what might happen later.

He swept her up and carried her toward the decadent, sumptuous whirlpool already filled and waiting. "Starting right now." He let her down slowly, sliding her body over the front of his.

As the starry, bliss-filled fantasy of a night wore on, Garrett was every bit as good as his promise.

I LOVE HIM, GRACE THOUGHT as she waved goodbye later the next morning to what she could see of him through the tiny plane window. *And I can't figure out how on earth it can ever work*. She never let any of that fear show, however, as she smiled and blew him kisses.

As his plane taxied away, Grace felt a part of her leaving with him. It was the oddest sensation, one she'd worked very hard to forget after Todd died, how someone could become such a part of you that you felt incomplete without them.

Oh, Garrett... When his plane became only a dot above the horizon, still she didn't move, caught in memories of a night like none she'd ever experienced. Dreams were made of such moments, and few women ever had the opportunity to be held in the arms of a man like him. By turns tender and nearly savage, he had made love to her as though he knew, as she did, how fragile their bond was, how newborn and delicate, easily snapped.

"Mommy! Mommy, I missed you!"

Grace turned at the sound of Bella's voice, to see her youngest and her father wreathed in smiles. She ran to them, gathering Bella to her, wishing Millie and Matthew weren't at school. "Oh, I've missed you, too." She wallowed in the soothing feel of her hugs and kisses, the almost audible snap of her life connecting again to its base.

Here was reality. Here was her purpose.

Last night had been an exquisite confection, a dream within a dream...but here was solid ground. Here was her life.

"Daddy." She rose and went to him, big and steady and beloved. "Thank you. I—oh, Daddy, what would I do without you?" When he enfolded her in his arms, she tucked her head into his shoulder and fought back tears.

"Hey, punkin, what's this?" His eyes narrowed. "What did he do?"

"You've been talking to Ethan and Jared. Don't listen to them. Garrett did nothing wrong. He was wonderful. It's just that—oh, Daddy, I'm afraid I love him," she whispered where her daughter couldn't hear.

He held her away from him a little and studied her face. "Would that be so bad?"

"I don't know. I just…" She wiped away the moisture and straightened. "I can't see how it can work. We're so different. And he's not a family man."

"Well, he'll have to be," Dan said gruffly. "Or the boys and I will bar him from your door."

The mental image of her father and two brothers ranged in front of her house, shotguns at the ready, made her giggle.

"Tomi doesn't feel good," Bella said, slipping her hand into Grace's. "I think he misses you, too."

"Tomi told me he liked sleeping with me better," said her father. "We'd best go settle this right now."

As Bella giggled, Grace let her worries over Garrett go. He would be gone for at least a week, and by the time he returned, they'd both be thinking more clearly, not swept up in all the excitement and emotion of the end of the season. "I agree with Grandpop," she said. "Tomi has some explaining to do." Buoyed by the sound of her child's laughter, Grace hitched Bella onto her hip and walked with her father to the terminal.

"It's good to be home," she said, and meant every word of it.

HER FATHER HAD OFFERED to hang around for the afternoon so she could take a nap, but she'd sent him home. First, because he'd done so much already, and second, because she craved time alone to simply be in her home and resume normal life. Millie and Matthew would be home in a few hours, and Bella was having her quiet time. No more calling it nap time—she'd decided she was too old for a nap, never mind that she often started out reading and still wound up asleep.

Grace had finished unpacking, had put her clothes into the washer and was in the middle of figuring out what to fix for dinner, when the doorbell rang. She was surprised to see Detective Haines on her front porch, along with Jake McMasters and Mattie Clayton.

She froze.

"Ms. Winters, may we come in?" Jake McMasters asked.

Their expressions were so somber. Foreboding filled her. "This is about my mother, isn't it?" She stepped back. "Let me just call my family and—" Then she halted. "No, go ahead and tell me now, then I'll figure out how to tell them." Panic at their grave demeanor set in. "Whatever you think you've found out about her, you didn't know her, and I don't believe she would ever—"

"Grace," Mattie said gently, taking her elbow. "Please, let's just sit down."

Grace gathered her raveling wits and sought calm. "Of course," she said, donning her best hostess manners. "Would you care for coffee or tea or something?" She cast around for what else she might be able to offer.

"We're fine," said Mattie. "Want me to get you anything?" Her voice was so sympathetic that it only increased Grace's anxiety.

"No. Thank you, though." She gripped her hands in her lap. She hadn't seen Mattie since the harrowing scene with Tony. "What's going on, Mattie? Are you writing a story about my mother?" She couldn't help feeling betrayed.

"No, Grace. I wouldn't—"

Jake McMasters intervened. "This isn't about your mother—well, it is, but…" He exhaled and exchanged glances with the others. "I don't guess there's an easy way to say this."

"Say what? That you still think my mother was part of the Grosso kidnapping? I tell you she would never—"

He held up one hand. "That's part of it, yes, but we're here because we believe that you are Gina Grosso."

For an endless moment, Grace couldn't make sense of the words, as though a loud gong had sounded inside her head, blotting out her ability to hear or think.

"What?" She shook her head to clear it. "What are you saying?" She rose. "That's impossible. My mother is Linda

Willard Hunt." She walked across her living room, her thoughts scattering like pickup sticks. "My father was Jack Willard. He drove race cars." She turned on them. "You—it's a crazy idea. I know who my mother is…was."

All three faces wore expressions of discomfort and sorrow, but not one of them bore doubt. "Jack Willard died in an automobile accident in April of 1978. His two-month-old baby daughter, Grace, died with him," reported Haines.

She staggered from the blow of his words. "What? I don't understand."

"Will you sit?" He gestured to the chair she'd vacated.

"I'd rather stand, thank you." Though her knees had gone spongy.

"Linda Willard was a nurse in the maternity ward of the Nashville hospital where Patsy Grosso gave birth to twins in June of 1978."

"My birthday is in February," interrupted Grace.

He nodded. "The real Grace Willard was born in February of 1978. She died in April of that year in an auto accident with her father. We've found the death certificate," he added.

Grace wanted to clap her hands over her ears and order them out of her house, but she would force herself to listen to them, then she'd figure out how they were wrong afterward. So she remained silent.

"Linda Willard had moved to Nashville, best guess is to get away from the pain of her memories, so she never told anyone about her husband or child. She was doing temp work at the hospital, and Patsy still recalls how kind she was to her during the birth."

"She was a kind woman, a good woman. She'd never—"

"Grief makes people behave differently than they normally would," Mattie said, her eyes concerned.

"What's your part in this?" Grace demanded.

"She's the reason we figured all this out," interjected Haines in a warning tone, reaching for Mattie's hand in a manner much more personal than professional. "She had an intuition early on that the killing of Alan Cargill and the kidnapping of Gina Grosso were related."

"How could you possibly connect the two?"

"My reaction was the same," said Haines. "I thought Mattie had it all wrong, but she wouldn't give it up."

"I had a photo of you, Patsy and Sophia, taken after your charity cooking demonstration—remember?"

Grace frowned. "It was a busy night."

"You had a lot of people competing for your attention. Anyway, Tony grabbed my phone to look at the photos right afterward. His behavior seemed odd at the time, but it was only later when I had a chance to really look at the pictures that I saw the startling resemblance among you, and my hunch seemed much more sound."

"So I reinterviewed your brother-in-law Tony," Haines said, "and he recanted his earlier story that he killed Alan Cargill for the money he could get from Cargill's jewelry."

"I don't understand."

"Turns out Tony suspected you were Gina Grosso for a while."

"No." Grace backed up, felt her legs hit a chair and sank into it. "No. How could he?"

"Because he heard Linda's confession to his mother, Susan, and started digging. When he uncovered Grace Willard's death certificate and evidence that Linda had worked in the hospital where Gina was born, he put two and two together."

"What does that have to do with Alan Cargill?"

"When you and Cargill talked at the banquet last year, do you remember asking him if he knew your dad, Jack Willard?"

"Sort of."

"Well, apparently that started Alan puzzling, because he recollected that Jack Willard's baby died in the accident with him. Best we can reconstruct, Alan was in that stairwell because no one could get a good signal inside the ballroom and he was trying to call Milo Grosso to see if his memory of that time jibed with Alan's own. Tony heard your conversation, too, and followed Alan down the stairs."

"Tony said he was after Alan's jewelry because he was desperate for money to settle gambling debts. What does that have to do with me?"

"Tony had decided to sell the information that you're Gina to the Grossos for a lot of money. Cargill talking to anyone would mess up his plan."

She was appalled. "Dear God." She wrapped her arms protectively around her waist. "This can't be. You have to be wrong. I have a family. I don't want this."

"You have another family that's missed out on thirty years with you."

She rocked a little. "I—I can't think about that right now." She looked up. "Tony's one thing. He's proven me a fool over and over for trusting him. But my mother…"

"Here's the best we can reconstruct," Haines offered. "Your—er, Linda Willard was suffering from depression after losing her daughter. The Grossos had two babies, one of them a girl. Maybe she thought that they had two and could spare one—we'll never know for sure. The records show that she burned herself on the ward and went to the emergency room for treatment, and she was sent home to recuperate. Before she left the hospital, she slipped into the nursery during a busy time and took Gina with her."

"No one noticed?"

"Apparently not, and she didn't return to work after the week she'd been told to lay off work to heal. The police questioned her during that week, along with everyone else who'd worked in maternity, but the records in the emergency room indicated that she'd been sent home at eleven o'clock, and baby Gina had been with Patsy in her room until eleven-fifteen, so there was no reason to suspect her."

"So why do you?"

"Because Linda Willard showed up three years later in Charlotte with a daughter born in 1978."

"But the wrong month." She had another thought. "I have a Social Security card. Surely that's proof that I'm Grace."

All three faces bore identical expressions of pity. "Those are not accepted as complete proof of identity because they can be faked too easily. More so in the past, but it still happens. In your case, she'd have likely provided the birth certificate for Grace Willard to obtain your card."

"But you said there's a death certificate for her, too. Wouldn't someone have noticed that?"

"The Social Security Death Index is about ninety-five percent complete nowadays, but the percentage has been considerably lower even in the recent past. It's not foolproof."

Grace rose again, suffocating on the information. Especially after Ethan's news that her mother had been a nurse. "I can't make it fit. She wasn't like that. You can't—" Then she fell still, remembering what Ethan had said, that Jake wanted to get DNA proof.

She whirled. "Are you here to get a DNA sample from me?"

"If you need the proof," Jake said.

"Of course I do." She thought desperately. "I can refuse, right? You can't make me."

"I can't, no. But don't you want to know for sure?"

Her heart was going to explode out of her chest. "My family," she murmured. "This is going to kill them." *It's killing me already.* "How can I tell them when I don't understand myself?"

Mattie approached her slowly, reaching for her. "Grace, take a deep breath."

"Don't touch me." She backed away, desperate to flee this news. "I have to think. I want you to go."

Haines's voice was deep and calm. "The test is very simple. It will take a second, literally." He held up a box with two plastic envelopes. "All I need is a swab from inside your cheek. Surely you want to know for certain."

He sounded so matter-of-fact. She wanted to rail at him for being callous, wanted to throw him out, all of them.

"We can come back later," he said. "But you'll only prolong the agony for everyone. The Grossos have suffered for thirty years."

It was then that she recalled Patsy's expression at the championship celebration and felt her heart sink as a new explanation occurred to her. "Do they know? Dean and Patsy?"

Jake nodded.

Grace put a hand over her throat. "How long?"

"A few days."

"Why hasn't anyone said something to me before?"

"You were already in Florida. They—it was hard for them to wait, but they didn't want you to find out when you were far from home."

"I thought you weren't going to get their hopes up until you were sure."

"That's my fault," Mattie said. "I'm working with Milo on his autobiography, and I was interviewing Patsy one day when Lucas called to tell me he'd interviewed Linda's landlord in Nashville, and he happened to mention that he hadn't known she would have a child there when he rented to her. He had a strict policy against children, but she explained that she was only taking care of her sister's baby for a few weeks while her sister had surgery. She left town not long after, and he didn't think about it anymore. Anyway, apparently Patsy heard enough of Lucas's voice through my phone to begin putting pieces together, and, well, she's my godmother, and she's suffered so much all these years. Even when everyone told her she had to put her baby's death behind her, without a body to bury, she was never fully at peace. Imagine spending thirty years wondering what your baby's last days were like, if she'd suffered, if she'd cried for you—"

"Stop." Grace was a mother, too. She could only too easily imagine Patsy's grief. "I—I can't—I don't want to think about this." But she did think about it, how that would feel. Thirty years… "All right. Do the test. Then please—*please* go away and leave me alone." As Haines neared with the test kit, she held up her hand, staring at Mattie. "How do I know I won't be reading about this in tomorrow's paper? It's a juicy story."

Mattie looked stung. "We've known each other for years, Grace. After what we went through with Tony, after all you've been through the last few years, how could you think I would?"

"You're a reporter."

"Even if I were so callous, Dean and Patsy have been my family. I've never had one of my own, not really. My mother's on her fourth marriage, and my half siblings aren't close. I owe Dean and Patsy so much, and I care about you. I'm not saying I wouldn't love to have an exclusive when this does break, but that's not a condition of my silence."

That nearly broke Grace. "I already have a family I love. I can't bear to lose them." Misery filled the air, some of it theirs, and she just wanted away from all of it. "Just do it. Then let me be."

"Open your mouth, please," requested Haines.

She complied, and he swiped one swab, then a second.

He stepped back, sealing them into a container. "Thank you."

An uncomfortable silence pulsed in the room.

Go, please go. Before I lose it.

"Mommy, the big hand is on the six and I can get up now," Bella called out.

Oh, God. "Please. I can't—"

"Expedited, it'll take about seventy-two hours," Haines said. "In case you wanted to know."

"Fine. Please leave now. I don't want to have to explain—" Her voice broke.

Mattie stroked her arm in comfort as she passed. Grace wanted to fall down and weep.

"Mommy?"

But she had a family to take care of. Even if everything else in her world was falling apart. "I'm in here, honey. Go potty, then I'll give you a snack." She sucked in a deep breath and made her way to the kitchen like a blind woman.

CHAPTER FIFTEEN

GARRETT RODE THROUGH the insanity that was Manhattan traffic, grabbing once again for the only contact with Grace that his tightly scheduled appearances would allow until later tonight: text messaging. He'd far rather talk to her, but it would be too frustrating to connect for only a couple of minutes when he had so much to say to her. He'd save calling her for tonight when they wouldn't be interrupted.

He sent the texts, however, understanding that he still might not get through to her. Grace wasn't big on keeping her phone with her when she was at home. The fact that he hadn't received a response to his earlier message probably meant that she was busy with the kids.

But he still missed her. Wished she were here with him, that at the end of this long day, he could know that she'd be waiting for him, arms open as they had been last night.

Man, he was so gone over her. He'd never experienced a night like the one he'd just passed. He'd missed more than a little sleep, yet even through the drain of interview after interview, there was a hum of eagerness inside him he hadn't felt in a very long time.

Of course, winning the trophy was part of it. He wasn't sure he'd ever get blasé about holding that gorgeous piece of metal. It was the culmination of years and years, since he was a kid, really, of busting his buns and grabbing every chance at seat time he could scrape up. The championship was validation of a sort that life didn't often hand most people. The trophy was evidence that he could look at for the rest of his life and know that he'd been to the top of the mountain.

He already wanted to repeat as champion next season. Thanks to this win and the money and acclaim that would come with it, he'd have a ride again next year, and a lot of people would still have jobs. Plus Andrew had bragging rights over the Grossos, at last. His stepdad was in New York, too, sometimes at the same stops, and years seemed to have fallen from his face. Man, that made Garrett feel good.

There was no denying, however, that Grace played a huge part in how life seemed brighter and filled with hope now. Much as he'd like to, he wouldn't win a championship every year.

But if he played his cards right, he could have Grace every day, every night, for the rest of his life.

Holy cow. The astonishing part was that he wasn't freaking out at the prospect of committing himself to a woman with three children. Him, the guy who'd sworn he never wanted a family at all.

He looked at his phone again, even though the signal for an incoming text remained stubbornly silent. "How much longer till we're done for the day?" he asked his PR escort.

"Miles to go before we sleep, my man," she said.

He sighed. "I was afraid of that."

He'd just wait to try again until he was free, and he could actually talk to her.

But man, he really did miss her.

Somehow she made it through after-school snacks and homework, dinner and baths and getting clothes ready for the next day.

As Grace made one more round of the children's beds, smoothing covers and bestowing kisses and hugs, the sweet simplicity of her children's love nearly undid her. They'd been full of stories of all the fun things they'd done with

Grandpop and Aunt Hope while she, Jared and Ethan were in Florida. Alight with the love of a supportive, nurturing family.

A family that might not be theirs, after all.

She walked to her bedroom on unsteady legs, beginning to shake as she had not allowed herself to do while with her children. She sank to the mattress, rolled to her side and curled against the nausea that had dogged her ever since she'd opened her front door to three people who'd blasted her world to bits.

Tomi leaped up and nuzzled her hair, purring loudly.

The tenderness broke her last restraint, and Grace began to cry, drawing the cat close, needing the warmth. She turned her face into the mattress to keep her children from hearing her sobs.

She kidnapped me. Her mother…who wasn't her mother after all? What was she supposed to think? How should she feel?

Anger ripped through her. Misery was a gnawing ache.

How could you do that, steal someone's baby? However much she didn't want to believe Jake and the others, she'd been lying when she said she didn't put herself in Patsy's place. Ever since they'd left, when she'd looked at one of her children, all she could think about was what if someone had done that to her, stolen one of them. To do that was to rip a mother's heart from her body, to ravage her soul and leave her empty.

She was sick over what Patsy and Dean must have suffered, but she didn't want this news to be true. She couldn't bear to lose the only family she knew. Worse, there was no one she could tell. The very people she'd normally go to when her heart was breaking, the ones who'd stood by her through the darkest hours of her life, were the ones who'd be hurt most by this news. She would not utter one word about this until someone gave her proof positive.

She longed to go to her father, to crawl up in his lap as the little girl Grace had done, spilling out her sorrows, content in the knowledge that he could and would fix whatever troubled her.

He hadn't been able to fix all her hurts when Todd died, of course, but he and her mother had stuck by her, just as she'd done everything she could for them when her mother got so sick and eventually left them. That was what family did, she'd always believed.

Now she was being told that her whole life was a lie, that all they'd shared, every bit of that powerful sense of belonging with Dan and Ethan, Jared and Hope, was an illusion.

She felt utterly alone. Of all she'd had to bear in the past few years, this was the hardest. She wasn't sure she was strong enough. "Help me hold on, Tomi," she murmured into his fur, trying to block out everything but his warmth and the solace of his purring.

When the phone rang, she considered not answering. She'd had enough of this day that had begun so beautifully, bright with promise after her incredible night with Garrett.

Garrett. She bolted up straight and looked at caller ID.

It was him.

But she wasn't the woman he'd left that morning. He was on a high in Manhattan, relishing the joy of his win, and she didn't want to dim that happiness, not for a moment, however desperately she wanted to hear his voice. When the ringing stopped, she tried to convince herself it was for the best.

But when her cell phone rang and it was him again, she told herself she could talk to him without loading her sorrows on his shoulders, just enjoy the respite from thinking. "Hello?"

"I miss you like crazy," he said.

Despite all her resolve, she started crying.

"GRACE? HONEY, WHAT'S WRONG?" Garrett shot up to sitting on the bed in his hotel room. This wasn't like cool, collected Grace at all. Then a stab of fear hit him. "Is it the kids? Did something happen to one of them?"

"No," she answered brokenly. "I'm sorry. They're all fine."

"Is it your family, then? Or you—are you all right?"

"No—yes. Oh, Garrett, I'm sorry. Never mind me." She sniffed. "I'm okay. What's—how has your day been?"

"Uh-uh. We're not doing that *never mind* bit. Talk to me. You don't cry easily. What's going on?"

The very long silence had him deeply concerned. "Grace?"

"I—" She cleared her throat. "I'm so glad you called."

He smiled at that. "You haven't had your phone with you, have you?"

"Why?"

"If you'll look, you'll see more than one text from me during the day. I could never get a long enough break to call you until now, but I…man, I wish you were here."

"It's great, though, isn't it? Exciting to be in demand—oh! I just realized you're on TV tonight, right? I want to watch. It's almost time."

"Forget that. Or record it. Talk to me instead. The real me. I miss you, Grace."

"I miss you, too." Her voice trailed off.

"I can't believe I have to wait a whole week to see you."

Another silence. "Garrett, I've been thinking. Maybe we shouldn't…"

"Uh-uh. Too late for the *we're not suited* conversation. I'm done with that." But he had a moment's hesitation, a sinking in his gut. "Are you trying to tell me what happened between us didn't matter?"

"I…"

"Screw that. I love you, Grace Hunt Winters. And damn it, I wanted to be with you when I said that."

"Oh, Garrett…" Soft sobs punctuated her breathing.

"Why do I not think those are happy tears?" he asked, trying for lightness even as his heart hurt. When she didn't respond, he fought a sense of betrayal. This wasn't how it was supposed to work. He'd gone and fallen in love with her, and she was supposed to love him. "I shouldn't have called."

"It's not…" A pause. "We didn't have much sleep last night. You need to be fresh for tomorrow."

Garrett had no practice with being dumped. He didn't like

it one bit. This hurt. Fury rode to the rescue. "We're not done, Grace. I'm not letting you go like this. If you're going to ditch me, you're going to do it to my face."

"I'm not…it's only that they…" She cut off whatever else she might have said. "Let's just say good-night, okay?"

Had she ever sounded so broken? "Grace, what's going on?"

"Get some sleep, Garrett. And enjoy your day tomorrow. I really mean that."

He wanted to say a thousand things, too many of them born of anger and hurt and bewilderment, but he would not lash out, and he refused to beg. "Tell the kids 'hi' for me." Probably a low blow, bringing up her kids, but he didn't feel all that charitable at the moment.

"I will," she said coolly. "Good night, Garrett."

He didn't answer, only hung up instead.

Then he stared out at the Manhattan skyline, wrestling with a boatload of conflicting emotions, knowing sleep was only a distant prospect.

GRACE CLUNG TO HER CELL PHONE, wishing she could start over. She hadn't meant to drive him away, but how was it fair to him to get more involved when she had no idea who she was? They were already so different. How could she pile on these miseries when he should be having the time of his life?

I love you, Grace Hunt Winters.

Oh, God. She couldn't—she wasn't ready…. Her head sank into her hands. Grace Hunt Winters might not even exist. However much she wanted to deny the truth of Mattie's bombshell, here, in her private thoughts, she had to admit that the evidence seemed overwhelming.

So what was she supposed to do about all this? How should she feel?

Lost, was all she knew. Unmoored and heading out to sea so fast she couldn't think, she had reacted by shoving away the helping hand of a man who had opened his heart to her. After exercising patience and control all evening, being there for her children, not calling her father or her siblings—and, blast it, she was going to call them that because that's what they were, DNA be hanged—what had she done?

She'd taken Garrett's words of love and hurled them right back in his face. He didn't deserve that. She'd been so happy when she'd heard his voice—didn't it say something that he was the only person she'd fallen apart in front of?

I love him, she'd admitted to herself just that morning. And he'd said he loved her, words she hadn't expected to hear for a long time, if ever.

So why was he in Manhattan and she in Charlotte, both miserable? She picked up her phone to dial.

It rang before she could.

"I'm sorry," she answered.

"I'm not giving up that easily," he said at the same instant.

Grace smiled, and felt herself steady for the first time since she'd opened the door to Jake McMasters. "I love you, too."

"That's not fair. We should be naked, or at least in the same room this first time." But he sounded better, too.

"I'd like that. Let's pretend we didn't say it."

"Not a chance. Now tell me what's wrong."

"I don't…you should be celebrating."

"Screw that. Talk to me, honey."

The tenderness in his voice reached down inside her and suddenly she didn't feel so alone anymore. "It's a long story."

"I've got all night."

So Grace began talking.

"I'M COMING HOME," he declared when she'd finished.

"You can't. You have all those commitments."

She was right, and he couldn't begin to imagine the consequences, but he'd figure something out. "I'm not leaving you to deal with all this alone, Grace. Don't even think it."

"It's your career, Garrett. Your sponsors and Andrew will be furious. You have to stay. I'll be fine."

Everything in him strained to go to her, to wrap her up and protect her. "You're not fine."

"I will be."

"You cried, Grace. *Cried.*"

A small laugh. "And now I feel better."

"That makes absolutely no sense."

He could hear her smile. "You're a guy. You don't get it." She hesitated. "I'd love nothing better than to be with you, but—"

"But nothing. It's a done deal."

"No, listen to me. I can handle this because of you, because I know you're there. I'm strong, but I was falling apart until you called me. Just knowing you care makes me stronger."

"That's not enough!" Frustration boiled over. "Grace, I just told you I love you. Doesn't that mean anything?"

"It means everything."

"Then let me be with you, take care of you."

"You know it's the wrong thing to do. People are counting on you."

He did, but he didn't have to like it. "This is wrong."

"This is love. Don't go all caveman on me. I'm a capable woman."

"Who cried."

"And likely will again, so deal with it." The smile was back. "Love is messy, Garrett. I'm beginning to think you're a romantic. An idealist."

"Get out." His cheeks felt hot. "I am not."

"You are." Her laugh was delighted. "Anyway, I like that about you." She sighed dreamily. "I keep remembering the penthouse suite and all the flowers and the music…the rose petals…"

"You liked it, huh?"

"It was the most romantic thing anyone's ever done for me."

Even your husband? he wanted to ask, and therein lay a new complication, dealing with the knowledge that he wasn't the first man she'd ever loved. With effort, he bit back the question. "I'm glad." He paused. "Man, I want to be back in that room."

"Me, too." Her wistfulness brought him back to reality.

"Grace, I can't stand thinking about you dealing with this all alone."

"I'm not alone. I have you now."

"I always ran as fast as I could from women saying things just like that. Funny how good it sounds."

"We're still really different. Let's not get ahead of ourselves."

"In four days, I'll be back in Charlotte. Don't expect me to take anything slow. I'm a guy who likes to go fast, remember."

"Not always." Scorching memories were in her tone.

His entire body reacted. "No, not always."

"Don't make me any promises, Garrett. I'd be lying if I said I wasn't lost right now. I have no idea how to deal with all of this. Can we just take things one day at a time?"

"That's supposed to be my line, Miss Grace," he drawled. "My, how you have turned my world on its head."

"You're teasing, but I'm serious. I was so overwhelmed, feeling so terribly alone, and then you called, just when I was wishing I could talk to you. That's an amazing thing, to know you're there for me."

"I am, Grace. Never doubt it."

She hesitated. "Thank you for not lecturing me about Patsy. I know you care about her. It's not that my heart doesn't go out to her, but…it's that she doesn't feel like my mother. What if she never does? Patsy's a good woman, and I've always liked her. I don't want to disappoint her, but I can't just suddenly love her because I'm supposed to. As a mother, though, I try to put myself in her place, and I know it would kill me for my child to say that."

"Want me to talk to her for you?"

She hesitated. "The coward in me says yes, but no. I have to do it myself. Part of me wants to wait, in case they're wrong."

"I never connected it, but I think your eyes are both blue." He paused. "Oh, weird. Kent's your twin brother."

"You're telling me. Not that there's anything wrong with him."

"Except the size of his ego."

She burst out laughing. "Right, Mr. Low Self-Esteem. You know nothing about being cocky, of course."

It was good to hear her laughing again, even if it was at his expense. "Grace, let me come."

"You know you have to stay there. You've helped so much, though. I'll be all right, I swear it."

That changed nothing. "Keep your cell with you, would you? And promise me you'll call the second you need me?"

"So, what—you'll ask the TV cameras to just hang on while you talk to me?" The teasing in her voice was a welcome sound.

"In a heartbeat. Of course, I'll be dead two seconds after I walk off the set because Sunny will have strangled me."

"Turn your phone off during interviews. If I need to get in touch, it won't kill me to wait until you're free."

"Promise me you'll call, even if it's just to talk."

"I will."

He wasn't sure he believed her, but he didn't push.

He was already making plans to be back in Charlotte the next night. She was right—he had to complete this media tour and take care of his responsibilities. He would do that, and do it well.

But nothing said he couldn't use his free time at night to see her. He could sleep on the plane. The notion settled him. He was a man of action, not sitting around waiting.

CHAPTER SIXTEEN

THE NEXT MORNING, after dropping Bella off at her preschool, Grace pulled into a shopping center parking lot a few blocks away and made the call she'd thought about all night.

"Cargill-Grosso Racing," said the receptionist.

"Is Patsy Grosso available? This is Grace Winters."

"I believe she is, but let me check."

Two beeps as she was put on hold. Grace's fingers trembled on the phone. She drew a deep breath and tried to calm her gyrating stomach.

In a matter of seconds, Patsy's voice came on the line. "Grace?" Normally unflappable, Patsy sounded nervous, too.

But Grace didn't want to get into all of this on the phone. She'd considered just showing up, but manners drilled into her by her mother—should she call her Linda now?—prevented that. Oh, God, this was hard. She pressed her lips together before proceeding. "Is it possible you might have time to meet this morning? It's short notice, but Bella's in school only until—"

"Of course," Patsy responded in the middle of Grace's dithering. "Shall I come to your house?"

She'd been too worked up to think about the place. "My—" She'd started to say *my family.* "People sometimes just drop in." And she wanted to be able to leave if she needed to.

"Milo and Juliana are gone for the day. We could have privacy at the farm, or I can meet you somewhere."

"The farm would be fine." And being there would give

Grace a chance to view a place she'd been before, catering a party, through new eyes. "Would thirty minutes be too soon?"

"I'm leaving right now. I'll be there in ten," Patsy responded. "Grace…"

Please don't say anything I'm not ready for. "Yes?"

"This has to be hard for you, and I'm so sorry."

Tears pricked at her eyes. The woman Grace had called mother had stolen Patsy's child, and Patsy was apologizing to her? "I'm the one who should—"

"You most certainly should not. You're the innocent in all this," Patsy said firmly. "Grace, I—"

Grace waited to hear the rest.

"Never mind. I'll see you in a few minutes. And thank you—" Her voice wobbled. "Thank you so much."

Grace didn't know how to respond. She didn't know anything at all right now. Especially the etiquette of meeting your mother when you were thirty-one years old.

WHAT THE GROSSOS CALLED the farm was something grander, a sprawling colonnaded Old South-style plantation house reached only by passing through stone pillars at the wrought-iron front gate, then weaving through the woods until suddenly the house, with its broad open porch, became visible.

Grace parked in the circular drive out front and paused for a moment to steady herself. *You can do this,* she told herself. And hoped she wouldn't make a mess of things.

When Patsy opened the door, Grace couldn't help searching for any resemblance. Patsy's hair was light brown and swung in a sleek straight bob to her shoulders where Grace's hair was blond and wavy. Patsy's hairdo was relatively new, however—she'd once worn her hair in what might have been natural curls. Garrett had been right that her eyes were blue.

Hungrily, Patsy's gaze also roamed over Grace, her smile too bright, a sheen of moisture in her eyes. "Please…please come in."

"Thank you." So formal, so polite, but Grace's insides were shaking.

As she passed, Patsy reached toward her but quickly drew back, pressing that hand to her side as if restraining herself from making contact. "Would you like some coffee or tea or…anything?"

"No, thank you. I'm fine," Grace responded, looking about her. The house was spacious, yes, and had been built with quality components, but the overwhelming aura was one of warmth, a feel to it that said home, not showplace.

It wasn't her home, though. And she couldn't imagine ever feeling differently. Aware of her extended silence and Patsy's own restraint, she turned. Equivocating wasn't like her. "I don't know how to do this," she admitted. "If it's true," she added hastily.

Patsy's look was all that Grace remembered from the celebration party at Homestead—uncertainty mixed with joy, overlain by yearning. "Do you think it's not?" Her composure faltered. "You and Sophia have the same mouth, the same coloring, and your forehead is like Kent's and Dean's. Your eyes are exactly the color of mine." She pressed her lips together. "I'm sorry. You're not ready." She gestured to a sofa. "Please…would you like to sit?"

Would she? "I don't know what I want, Patsy. To wake up and find out all this is a dream? That I don't have to give up my fam—I'm sorry. That hurts you, and I don't want to. You're a good woman, and this has to have been hellish for you. I—I don't know how I could have survived it."

"You just do. Especially when you have another child to take care of—I know you understand this. You've been through something just as terrible, being widowed so young and with three little ones, but you didn't let it defeat you. I admire you, Grace."

"You…do?"

"Absolutely. Look at what you've accomplished. Left with

small children and no job, you've carved out a very success-ful career, and from what I've seen of your children, your success hasn't come at their expense, either."

"I hope not. I try very hard, but my fam—"

"It's all right." Patsy's smile was fond, if sad. "They're still family. I don't expect you to forget all the years you've had together."

"She was wrong to do it." Grace could give Patsy that much. "My—Linda. If she stole your baby, that's totally un-forgivable. I just don't know how to square this with the mother who was so good to us. Though I guess you don't want to hear that she was a good mother." She'd never felt so all-thumbs in her life.

"Would you not want your children to be well loved, in my place? Even if it was someone else caring for them? I lay awake nights wondering what Gina felt, if she was hurting or hungry or—" Patsy clamped her lips together. Blinked rapidly.

"It must have nearly killed you. I am so sorry," Grace whispered. "I don't know how to fix this. How to feel or what to do or—"

Patsy stepped toward her, arms rising from her sides hesi-tantly. "Grace, may I…just as a friend, as someone who cares…"

"We don't know yet, not for sure." It was cruel to say that, when Patsy so obviously ached to hold her, but everything inside Grace was such a mess.

Patsy swallowed hard and let her arms fall. "I'm sure," she said, wiping her eyes. "But I understand that it's more diffi-cult for you. Dean and I—all of us—have everything to gain, yet all you must feel is what you're losing."

She was so compassionate. Grace looked at this woman who'd never been anything but kind to her, who was obviously hurting yet determined to respect Grace's own wishes, and in that moment, Grace could not respect herself for wanting so badly to find out it was all a mistake. But she did, desperately. "Could we just…I'm really sorry. I shouldn't have come.

I'm—I'm having a hard time, but it's my fault, not yours. You're a wonderful woman. I—I've always liked you a lot." Her voice petered out. "That's such a stupid thing to say."

A watery smile. "No, no, it's not." Gingerly Patsy touched Grace's arm. "Liking is a better start than I have any right to expect. This must be such a terrible shock for you."

Grace thought at that moment that if Patsy were indeed her biological mother, she could not ask for better genes, so gracious and understanding and, well, motherly, Patsy was by nature. "You deserve much better. You're the person who was harmed so grievously. You must have suffered so. When I think of what it would be like to lose—"

"Don't torment yourself, Grace, please."

"But I feel like I need to make up to you for what she did."

"What *she* did, remember that. Not you." Patsy studied her for a minute. "How about we change the subject for now, give us both a chance to settle? May I make you a cup of coffee, please? And perhaps you could tell me some stories about those lovely children—or whatever you'd like to talk about," she revised hastily.

Grace realized suddenly that if all this was true, her children would be Patsy's only grandchildren, at least thus far. Kent and Sophia were both newly married.

She would be a good grandmother, Grace thought, resisting the pang that accompanied the notion of Dan's claim as grandfather being replaced by Dean's.

They're still family, Patsy had said. *I don't expect you to forget all the years you've had together.*

She couldn't. Didn't want to. But could children ever have too many people caring about them? "Millie's very shy, and she took Todd's death so hard. I'm still worried about her, though she is opening up more all the time."

Patsy seemed to understand that Grace was trying. "She's your middle child, right? With that lovely dark hair?" She gestured toward the kitchen then turned to lead the way.

"Yes. She's six, Matthew is eight and Bella, my handful, is four. But sixteen in her heart. And in charge."

Patsy laughed. "Oh, I hear you. Sophia managed to marry the heir of our family's mortal enemy, but I'd already had years of practice dealing with that very hard head of hers."

Grace followed right behind her. "I take cream but no sugar."

Patsy closed her eyes for a second, then smiled as though the sun had brought out the morning.

SHE STAYED FOR NEARLY AN HOUR. The leave-taking was less awkward than the arrival, but not much. None of that was Patsy's fault. Though she clearly wanted Grace to stay longer, to be happy about the possibility of being her daughter, she very carefully did not push.

Which only made Grace feel worse that she couldn't simply embrace the notion that she was Gina Grosso.

Oh, lordy—would they expect her to change her name? Her stomach dropped to her feet when that thought occurred to her. That and too many other questions rocketed around in her head until she knew she couldn't go to the shop. She wanted to crawl into a cave somewhere and hide from everything.

But she had children to care for. A business to run, a future to make for herself and her children and her employees.

And then there was Garrett, a complication all his own.

She decided to work at home and lose herself in paperwork. When that only used up an hour, she moved on to tidying up the house, but doing so was only physical effort and allowed her brain too much time to think.

Finally, she resorted to what always soothed her in times of trouble: she cooked. She began with bread, taking great pleasure in the nutty aroma of the yeast, the sticky-smooth texture of the dough as she kneaded it. When it was in the bowl to rise, she had a yen for cassoulet, but the best ones required two days, so she settled for making a gumbo.

She'd invite her family over, as she'd promised Ethan. She would forget for one night that she might not be Grace Hunt Winters. They had never been blood kin, except her mother and Hope, anyway, but they were still her family.

But even Hope, it sank in now, would not be related, should the test results show that she was Gina Grosso. The ache nearly bent her double. Perhaps not a one of them shared her blood. For a moment, she couldn't breathe.

She sank into a chair, head in hands, too drained to move. She thought of the phone in her pocket and longed to use it, but she didn't know where Garrett was right now, and anyway, she had to come to grips with all of this on her own.

A tap on the back door window brought her head up.

The sight that greeted her had her running to open it. "What are you doing here?"

Garrett stepped inside and grabbed her. "I'm glad to see you, too." Then he wrapped her in his arms and lowered his mouth to hers.

And for the first time since she'd watched him fly away, Grace felt centered. Safe.

Home.

"Thank you," she murmured against his lips. "I needed you."

"I'm here, love," he answered. Then lifted his head. "Say it. I want to hear it while I'm looking at you. Holding you."

"Say what?" Grace stretched against him, all innocence, optimism flooding through her and making her playful when she'd thought she'd never feel lighthearted again.

"Chicken." His eyes turned serious. "I love you, Grace."

"What if I'm not Grace?"

"You're still you. Say it."

She touched his face. "I love you, Garrett." She rose to her toes and kissed him with all the tenderness she knew.

He swept her up in his arms and twirled her. "Again."

She couldn't help smiling. "I love you. I love you." She grew dizzy, and somehow her troubles were slung from her as though by centrifugal force. She would tell him about seeing Patsy, but not now. "Your turn."

"I love you, gorgeous." He slid her down the front of his body and nuzzled at her neck. "Where are the kids?"

"Huh?" She was floating. "What?"

"Children? Millie, Matthew? Bella?"

"Oh, them." She grinned. "At school."

His eyes went hot. "How long?"

She glanced at the clock. "Two hours."

"Not nearly enough time."

"I have bread rising."

His head lifted, scenting like a wolf. "Bread? Your bread?"

She swatted at his shoulder. "What happened to hot sex?"

"You do know how to make a man weep."

"The bread will have to be punched down in about an hour."

He grinned. Waggled his eyebrows. "Round one, then." He picked her up. "Where's the bedroom?"

"That way." She pointed while slicking her tongue up his throat.

Garrett groaned, long and low but never stopped walking until he'd found her bed.

The dough got punched down for its second rising.

But they were barely covered and giggling while they did it.

HER GUMBO INTENTIONS gave way to chicken vegetable soup assembled from ingredients she'd prepared and frozen earlier. As Grace finished cooking supper, she listened to the chatter behind her in the family room, smiling.

When she and Garrett had shown up to pick up each of the kids, she wasn't sure they'd even noticed her. Garrett was the star of the show. Bella had shrieked and leaped into his arms, and Millie had surprised her by reaching up to him for a hug. Matthew's friends had crowded around, peppering him with questions about the race and begging to see the trophy. Garrett had promised a viewing when he returned from New York, for which he had to depart later tonight. She could only imagine the maneuvering required to pull off this visit, but she was grateful.

"You're smiling."

She jolted at his voice while his arms slipped around her waist from behind. "It smells awesome." He sniffed elaborately at her neck and made her giggle. "I meant you, of course."

"That tickles."

"Tickling can be arranged, Miss Grace." His voice was both a come-on and a caress.

She was glad now that she hadn't had time to invite her family. She needed to have him to herself for whatever precious moments possible after the kids went to bed, until he had to get back on the plane.

"Behave yourself." She smacked his arm with a spoon. "I'm about to slice the bread. Would you tell the kids to wash their hands?"

"I will never look at a loaf of bread the same again." He winked.

She laughed and shooed him off.

And tried not to sigh out loud at the memories.

"I SAW PATSY THIS MORNING," Grace said as he was shrugging on his coat.

"What?" He whirled. "Why?"

She stiffened. "I have the right to do it."

"I'm sorry. That's not what I meant. I would have gone with you."

"I've been running my own life for a long time, Garrett. I don't need you to take care of me."

She was clearly upset. So was he. "Why did you wait until now to tell me?"

"I didn't—I don't—" She threw up her hands. "I don't know how to do this, any of this. I feel like my whole life is teetering on the edge of a cliff, so I'm sorry if I'm not properly handling your feelings."

He had a quick temper at the best of times. Now, when he was facing being away from her again and loathing the fact, was not one of those. "I'm not a hothouse flower, Grace. I don't need handling."

"Neither do I." If those had been real sparks in her eyes, he'd be singed right now.

Someone needed to be the cool head. At another time, he'd laugh his butt off to think he could be that someone. "Are we having our first fight?" He found a smile for her then.

"Hardly our first disagreement, unless you've developed amnesia." Humor returned to her, too.

"No, no, you're not getting the importance of this. We said we love each other, so that means we're a couple now, tonight, like officially. So this is our first official fight." He grinned. "Like a real occasion. We could write it in a book or something. You women like that, right?"

"Right," she drawled.

"So does this call for make-up sex?"

Finally she laughed. "You are incorrigible."

"Well, yeah…but does that mean no?"

"I believe there's a plane waiting to take off."

"Hey, but it's my plane. I get to call the shots." Finally he relented and drew her close. "Okay, but you owe me some make-up sex Friday night when I get home." He wrapped his arms around her and rocked gently. "I just want to take care of you, Grace. Neanderthal that might make me, but I want to protect you. It kills me that you have to go through this at all, and I just want to make it as easy as I can."

She hugged him hard. "You do. You have no idea how much. When I saw you at the door today—" she pressed her forehead into his shoulder "—it was like my own personal miracle."

Had a woman ever said anything to make him feel half so good? "Was it really hard seeing her, sweetheart?"

Grace's head nodded, but then she lifted it. "But that's not her fault. She's wonderful, Garrett. As kind and understanding as I could ever hope for."

"Aunt Patsy's always been terrific."

Grace winced. "I wish you wouldn't say that. It sounds like we'd be cousins."

"Kissing cousins, though…not half-bad," he teased. "You know she and I are not related by blood at all. I just grew up calling her that."

"I do…but it still makes me squirmy."

"Aw, come on, cuz." He nuzzled his nose into her throat and made her giggle.

"Stop that. You have to leave or—"

"Or what? You'll beg me to stay?"

Her eyes grew serious. "I shouldn't, but I wish you could."

"I can try—"

"No." She shook her head. "If we're to make this work, we have to respect the other's career and the demands of it." Her expression was somber. "Garrett, I'm a lot to take on. It's not just my business and my kids…it's all this family stuff, too. It could be a real mess."

"Well, bein's that I'm such a great bargain, so calm and easy, no baggage of my own and all…you're right. I'm obviously the one with the hardest job."

She tapped his chest. "This is serious."

He snagged that hand and brought it to his lips. "I know it is. What I'm trying to get through that thick head of yours— Bella is clearly yours, by the way—" He laughed when she frowned. "Is that however astonishing the notion, I might actually be grown-up enough to deal with more than just being a world-class driver and babe magnet."

Her lips curved as she looked at him, then exhaled strongly. "I'll stop worrying."

He laughed. "I seriously doubt it." Then he lowered his mouth to hers. "But I love how you are. I'm here for you, Grace. I wish I didn't have to leave tonight, and I refuse to go until you promise me you'll call me the second you need me, as often as you want."

"You could run out of minutes."

He brushed his lips over hers. "I'm about to collect a nice, fat pay check. I'll buy more." Then he poured himself into kissing her, soothing her, sealing a vow he meant from his soul.

To be what she needed. Whatever that meant.

CHAPTER SEVENTEEN

FOR THE NEXT TWO DAYS, Grace managed to stay busy. Fortunately, her workload increased as the holidays approached, and she also had to finalize plans for the cookbook's release in February. Garrett texted her often during the day, and they were on the phone for hours each night. She was extremely grateful that his junket provided ample fodder for amusing stories and that he did everything possible to distract her from worrying over when she'd get the test results and what they would show.

Lucas Haines had said seventy-two hours, but she didn't know where the lab was, when the samples had been turned in or what other factors would determine when she got the news. It was Friday, and she had no idea if the weekend would interfere, so she tried to focus on the fact that Garrett would be home tonight from New York and forget anything else.

But she would also see her father tonight—she couldn't call him Dan in her mind, no matter what. He was Daddy to her and had been since she was three. He was keeping the kids while she and Garrett had a real, live date. Garrett was being very mysterious about his plans, constantly dropping conflicting hints to keep her guessing, but she blessed him for that because it helped with her nerves over seeing her father for the first time since the bombshell had blown apart her life.

Her father was picking up Bella from school, but he would bring her home and wait for the other kids to arrive on the bus, then stay with them at the house, since the kids were clamoring to see Garrett when he arrived.

It came as no surprise that Bella believed she should be included in this date. "Garrett loves me, Mommy," she'd said with perfect assurance. "We could both marry him."

Grace couldn't repress a chuckle at the memory. Barbini glanced up from his work and smiled. Her staff had ribbed her unmercifully about the big-screen incident at Homestead. There had been a few awkward moments with Sarah when Grace first saw her and both obviously remembered that Garrett had first crossed Grace's path when he was kissing Sarah in the utility closet, but Sarah had readily admitted that Garrett had never looked at any woman the way he looked at Grace. Grace decided the better part of valor was to simply drop the subject.

Recalling her efforts to convince the world's most stubborn four-year-old that a) Grace wasn't marrying Garrett, just dating him, and b) they couldn't both marry the same person, brought another smile to Grace's face.

But he loves us and we love him had been Bella's response, and Grace knew better than to think that logic could dissuade her youngest when her mind was made up. She'd understand when she was older. Nonetheless, she'd broken the news to Bella that Grace and Garrett would be going out alone. Period.

The phone at her desk rang, and Grace picked it up, still smiling. "Grace Winters."

"Grace, it's Jake McMasters."

The bottom dropped out of her stomach. "It hasn't been seventy-two hours." *I'm not ready.*

"I'm in the parking lot across the street, but I didn't want to just drop in on you again. Can you meet me here? Or would you rather go to your house?"

"No," she said hastily. Her father—oh, God—might already be there. She thought madly. "I'll see you at the Italian place on the next block." She hung up and rose.

"Lover boy here already?" Barbini asked.

"No." Her voice was too sharp. Blast Jake for interrupting her here. "I, uh—it's just—" She couldn't say a supplier because Barbini knew all of them. If she said something to do with her children, her staff would worry. "It's—I have to meet a flooring guy at the house," she improvised. "See you all tomorrow at noon to start prep." They had a wedding to cater Saturday night.

"I've got it under control, Grace, if you want to take a pass on this one." Barbini was obviously concerned.

She shook her head. "I've been gone too much, but thanks." She barely remembered to grab her purse and coat as she rushed out.

Her hands were shaking as she gripped the steering wheel. For a minute, she was afraid to drive. *Pull it together, Grace. He could very easily be about to tell you that you're not Gina Grosso, then your life will settle right back down.*

She wished for that so much.

Yet she kept seeing Patsy's grief, her kindness…her longing. *Don't think. Just don't think.* She parked the car at the restaurant but didn't get out. Her hand hovered over her phone, but Garrett would be on his plane anytime now, she thought. Anyway, she had to handle this herself. She and Garrett were only an item, an affair…nothing solid.

There was nothing solid in her life, she realized, and she was terrified, more so even than when she'd found herself alone at twenty-eight. *No, not alone,* she lectured herself. *You have Matthew and Millie and Bella. Think of them.*

She emerged from the car and walked to the door, feeling as though she was about to meet the executioner.

"Grace." Jake's voice from behind her. "If you'd rather not go inside, we can sit in your car or mine."

Slowly she revolved to face him. Clenched her fingers over her keys. "Just tell me."

"You sure?"

"Jake, please. Don't drag this out."

"All right." He looked straight at her. "They tested your DNA against Patsy's. There's no doubt—you are Gina Grosso."

She closed her eyes, sagged against the car.

"Here," he said, gripping her arm and opening her door. "Sit down, Grace."

She complied because her mind was a whirlwind. Out of the chaos, she plucked one question. "It hasn't been seventy-two hours. It could be wrong."

"No. The test can require as little as twenty-four. They say seventy-two to allow for paperwork or delays, but Lucas Haines sent it to a lab where he has good connections."

Head bowed, she pressed one hand to her forehead and rubbed it back and forth, everything inside her freezing, unable to think, to know how to feel, to—

"Can I get you something, Grace? Call someone?"

Garrett, she wanted to say, but she couldn't have that. *Daddy or Ethan or...* She beat back the sob that wanted to erupt. "No, I just—oh, God, Jake, what am I going to do?"

"They're good people, the best."

"I know…I know, I do. But my mother—only she's not and she's a criminal and this is going to kill my—Dan and—" Ruthlessly, she brought herself under control. "I'm okay, Jake."

"I don't think so. What if we go inside and have coffee while it settles in?"

Kind as he was, Jake McMasters was not who she wanted to be with right now. "Thank you, but no. I'd better—" A sob broke through as she recalled that she should be getting home. How could she face anyone now?

"Let me drive you then."

"No, I'll just sit here until I'm calm. Please, I'd like to be alone. I—it's not your fault."

"I feel like it is."

"You didn't create this situation." And if she thought for one more second about who had, she'd go crazy. She drew herself up straight. "I've had worse news."

Chagrin rode his features. "Is this really so bad? They're over the moon."

Sweet mercy, she would have to see them. Figure out how to— "They'll want me to change my name," she blurted. Random thoughts flew like a hail of bullets in her head. Why on earth had she snatched that one?

"Grace, they're just happy you're alive. It's their miracle. Patsy asked me to tell you to take your time."

Tears threatened. "She would, wouldn't she? After all she's suffered. I should go see them, but—" At that moment, her phone rang. She had the impulse to throw it out the window, but a mother away from her children couldn't, of course. She snatched it up, saw that it was Garrett. Wondered if he was delayed. "Excuse me," she said to Jake. "Hello?"

"I'm at your office. Where are you? Everyone's worried."

"Garrett." Her voice faltered for a second. "Please…please come." Like an automaton, she handed the phone to Jake. Vaguely she heard his quick explanation and their location, then he closed her phone.

"He'll be here in just a second."

She nodded but couldn't speak. All she could do was hold on.

GARRETT HAD BEEN IN SOME hair-raising situations on the track, but never had adrenaline coursed through him like this. Grace sounded awful, and Jake was clearly worried. He wheeled into the parking lot and immediately spotted Jake crouched beside the open driver's door of Grace's car. He bolted from his car. "What the hell did you do to her?" It was all he could do not to shove Jake aside in his haste to get to her.

She looked terrible, so pale, so still. What the news had been was obvious. "Grace, honey, I'm here." He shot a glare at Jake, who held up his palms.

"I'm really sorry, man."

At last Grace turned to him, her big blue eyes pools of grief. "Garrett, how did you make it home so soon?"

He drew her gently to her feet and into his arms. "I wanted to surprise you."

She nestled against him, shivering. A watery chuckle. "A lot of surprises today," she murmured.

"Grace, I'm so sorry," Jake repeated.

"You can just get the hell out of here." Garrett was furious. He'd never seen her so destroyed.

She lifted her head. "It's not your fault, Jake." She seemed to be coming back to herself a little. "I don't imagine there's a manual on how to give news like that." She looked at Garrett. "He did it as kindly as he could."

She might be forgiving, but he couldn't, not yet. "Just go on, Jake—no, wait."

Jake had been about to turn away but halted.

"Do they know, Dean and Patsy?"

He nodded. "They're my clients."

"Tell them I'll call them later and work things out. I'm taking Grace home right now."

Grace made the return journey to the woman he knew. "You will not work this out for me, Garrett. I have to face them myself." She drew a ragged breath. "Please tell them, Jake, that I appreciate their understanding and will be in touch soon. I have to tell my fam—" Her voice wobbled, then firmed. "I have to tell Dan and his children first."

The pain of not feeling like one of those children anymore was written all over her face. "They're still your family, Grace. Patsy and Dean won't begrudge that."

She searched Garrett's eyes for the truth of it. "Even so, this is going to kill my—Dan and the others."

Jake's discomfort showed, but to his credit, he stayed where he was. "Garrett's right, Grace. One of the first things Patsy said was how grateful she is that you were loved all these years."

One hand briefly covered her mouth as tears started to spill, but Garrett watched as Grace pulled herself together. "She said as much to me the other day. Please don't worry, and tell them not to. I'll be all right. Really."

I'll make sure of it, Garrett vowed. She was the strongest woman—make that person—he'd ever known, but he wanted, more than anything, to convince her that from now on, she didn't always have to be.

"I'll do that," Jake said. "And again, I'm sorry if…"

"You did fine." She broke from Garrett's embrace and went to Jake, hand out to shake but then hugged him instead.

Garrett put his effort into not going all Neanderthal on her. Hugging Jake was a classy thing to do.

Even if he wanted to put a fence around her with a big, fat sign that said *Mine.*

"WHAT ABOUT OUR DATE?" Grace asked as they pulled up to her house, seeing her father's car already parked. *Dan's car,* she amended. "He won't want to stay."

"I wouldn't count on it, but anyway, forget the date. We can do it later."

"But you've been full of plans."

"Plans can change."

"But—"

"Let's do this. We'll go inside, and I'll take Bella somewhere. You and your dad can talk."

"That's not fair to ask of you."

"Grace, you've been through a shock, but I'm starting to get just a little ticked here. I know you're a capable woman, but would it kill you to let me help you?"

Chagrin washed through her. "I'm sorry. I'm not used to this, is all. The idea that someone…"

"Loves you, those are the words you're looking for. I love you, Grace."

"But we hardly know each other." Why was she doing this? *I'm scared, that's why. Any minute he's going to wake up and realize he's in over his head.*

He clenched his jaw. "I'm not arguing with you over this." He glanced at her. "Cut yourself some slack, honey." His tone gentled, and his eyes were warm caramel. "It's been a rough day, and you've barely begun." His grin was sunlight peeking through the dismal clouds.

"Boy, you're not kidding."

He reached for her hand. "We'll get through this. Remember, it's not like people are fighting over who has to take you. You're the prize, Grace. You have one family who already loves you and the whole Grosso clan just waiting for you to let them."

She pressed a palm to her stomach. "Thanks for reminding me. There's a thousand of them."

"At least." He lifted her hand to his lips, then squeezed it. "Whenever you're ready."

She glanced at her house. "Could we drive around the block?" But she summoned the shadow of a smile. "Kidding. Sort of."

"Garrett!" came the shout as the front door opened, and Bella burst outside.

Then Grace's smile was full and real. "Notice whose name is conspicuously missing from that greeting."

He lifted his shoulders. "Hey, can I help it if I'm catnip to women, even pint-sized ones?"

Then Dan Hunt stepped onto the porch with a wide smile, and Grace's smile faltered.

GRACE WAVED GOODBYE to Bella, regally ensconced in her car seat in Garrett's car and on her way for ice cream.

"What's wrong, punkin?" asked Dan, sensing without words, as he always had, when she was troubled.

She clasped her hands together and faced him. "Maybe we should sit down."

"Maybe you should, but I'm fine. What's up? Is it Clark? Has he—what's the deal with him, anyway? The kids can't talk about anything else."

"I—we can talk about Garrett later. This is—" Her heart was pounding so hard she was feeling faint. "This is about Mom."

"Go on," he said warily.

"I don't know how to say this, Daddy."

"Just spit it out." Dan Hunt was a direct man who confronted life boldly. "Have you learned something? Jared didn't tell me he'd heard from our investigator."

"Jared doesn't know." Her throat closed up, and she had to pause to get herself back together. "She did it, Daddy. She stole the Grosso baby."

"She *stole* it? All Susan said was that she'd played a part, not—she wouldn't have." His frame went rigid.

"I'm sorry, but the evidence is irrefutable. I didn't want to believe it myself."

"So why do you? What evidence?"

"Me." She fought to keep control. "I'm that baby. I'm Gina Grosso."

He looked as staggered as she'd felt. His mouth opened, then closed again. "No." He shook his head, tried again. "She wouldn't. Who's saying that?"

"A DNA test. I just got the results." As she watched his face radiate fury, she thought she couldn't bear it. "Daddy, I'm sorry. I wish it weren't so. I don't know what to do, and I can't stand for you to hate me or—"

He recoiled. "Why would I hate you? Honey, what on earth do you have to apologize for?"

Tears she was sick of spilled past her lashes, regardless. "I'm just so afraid. I love you and you've always been there and I don't know what I'll do without you."

Strong arms surrounded her, hugged her into the broad chest that had sheltered her all her life. Grace curled into him and wept out her misery, crying so hard that at first she couldn't make out his words.

"—would you ever have to do without me?" He drew back just a bit. "Grace, you were never the child of my blood, but that didn't matter one bit. It still doesn't. I adopted you, and I'm keeping you. We'll figure this out." He halted. "What have the Grossos said to you? I won't let them hurt you, DNA be damned."

For the first time in days, Grace drew a solid, steady breath. "I haven't spoken to them since I found out. I had to talk to you first."

"Well, of course you did. I'll go with you to see them, and we'll straighten all this out."

His indignation bolstered her. "Daddy—" she hesitated "—I don't care. I'll find something else to call Dean but you are my daddy."

"Damn straight."

She smiled. "Thank you."

"I'll kick anyone's ass for you, you know that."

"I do, but I meant thank you for not, I don't know, giving me up."

"Did you honestly think I would?"

"I don't know. I've been so confused." Then she remembered. "But, Daddy, I'm sorry, too. It must hurt you to know that about Mom. I can't understand it."

"It's a hell of a shock, I agree." He paused, thought for a minute. "There's no way to say she was anything but wrong to do it, but this explains a lot." At the expression Grace knew reflected her confusion, he continued. "She was never interested in talking about her past, not even to me, not from the first day. I was so taken by her that I didn't want to rock the boat. She'd get very agitated, and I guess I always thought she'd tell me one day, but that day never came." He shook his head. "Then she was gone. I guess we'll never really know why."

Grace hesitated, but the news would come out soon. Better he hear it from her. "I know why. She had a daughter who died."

His eyes widened.

"The real Grace Willard died at two months old. From what Jake and Lucas Haines uncovered, Mom—" she cast her eyes up at him "—I don't know if I can call her Mom, but Linda feels wrong, too."

"You just do what you need to, honey."

She nodded, then went on to detail the explanation she'd received from Jake and Mattie Clayton and Lucas Haines.

He listened to her all the way through, his shoulders sagging a little. When she finished, he sat in thought for a bit, then slapped his hands on his thighs and rose. "The boys and Hope will have to know. Your kids, too, and real soon, I'd guess. This will be a juicy story. It won't hold long."

Her heart sank. "I hadn't thought that far." She stared outside. "And I have to go see them, Patsy and Dean."

"I'll go with you."

She smiled and turned to face him. "I know you would. Garrett offered, too, but…can I ask you a favor, Daddy?"

"Anything, punkin."

"Would you still stay here for the kids? And tell Garrett where I am?"

"You're going now?"

She nodded. "I think I have to. No matter how little they feel like my parents, I can so easily put myself in Patsy's place and imagine what I'd do if I'd lost one of mine and found them again. They're good people, Daddy, and they've suffered a long time. They don't deserve me being a coward."

"You've always made me proud, Grace, but never more than now." He hugged her, and she rocked with him for a moment that helped restore her. "You go on, and I'll take care of things here. I'll call your brothers and sister and tell them, too, before Garrett and Bella get back. Don't want them to hear it from someone else."

"Do you think they'll… I don't want to lose them, either."

"Of course you won't, honey." He smiled. "But that man of yours is not going to be happy that you didn't wait for him."

"I don't know if he's my man. We're too new to each other."

He rolled his eyes. "Yeah, and a guy who isn't in it for the long haul just offers to take care of your child even as he's warning me I'd damn well better not hurt you."

"Oh, no. He shouldn't have said that."

"Of course he should. No man worth his salt won't go to the wall to protect his woman." Dan grinned. "Doesn't mean he won't be mad as hell at you for going ahead. Best be scootin' along."

"I guess so." Then she remembered. "My car's still in a parking lot. May I borrow yours?"

He plucked his keys from his pocket and pressed them into her hand. "You scratch it, you bought it." His old refrain to each of the kids as they began driving.

Grace laughed, flush with the joy of feeling connected for the first time all day. "I remember." She hesitated at the door. "Daddy, I love you so much."

He nodded. "And I love you."

CHAPTER EIGHTEEN

ONCE AGAIN, GRACE APPROACHED the farm feeling a bit as if a firing squad awaited. The day was chilly, but her palms were sweating and suddenly she wished she'd called first, after all. There were several cars in the driveway. They must have company. The timing was all wrong. She should turn around, but that wasn't so easy without driving onto the grass, and she wouldn't chance digging a rut.

Grace faltered, barely remembering to put the car in Park, and rested her head on the steering wheel. She was shaking and her thoughts were darting around like buzzing flies. How on earth would she ever—

A tap on the driver's window shot her heart straight into the red zone. She bolted upright.

And stared into the face of Dean Grosso. Her biological father. "Are you all right?" he seemed to be saying. She nodded, but the concern on his face brought her near tears again. She looked away, determined not to cry.

He opened the door slowly, then squatted next to her. "Can I do anything to make this better?"

She bit her lip and faced him. "I don't know." But at that moment, she spotted something that amazed her. "Matthew has your nose."

His face glowed like sunlight. "Really?" His eyes turned dreamy. "My…*grandson*. Is it okay for me to say that?"

She couldn't speak around the lump in her throat, so she only nodded.

His brow furrowed. "Would you come inside, Grace?"

"You have company."

"Just family. It's sort of a tradition to get together once the season's over and celebrate." A quick grin. "Or cuss…whatever's appropriate for that particular year."

His smile was infectious. "That's nice." A thought occurred to her. "So, since Garrett beat Justin, will this be a cussing year?"

He laughed, but then his eyes grew moist. "Because of you, nobody gives a hoot how the season went. Celebration is too mild to describe how we all feel." He reached for her hand. "How about you? Can you find a place for us in your heart, Grace?"

Her own eyes stung. Dean Grosso was renowned for being a fierce competitor and a man who shot straight from the hip. This man was more, gentle and kind and thoughtful. "Shouldn't you call me Gina?" A pang of terror rocked her loose from the few moorings she had left.

"What do you want to be called, sweetheart?" His hand was big and warm and comforting.

"I don't know." Tears spilled then. "I don't know much of anything right now."

"Here, now…" He drew her out of the car and started to hug her but halted. "Could I—may I—" Gingerly he slipped an arm around her shoulder.

She leaned a little into the comfort. "I am so sorry for all you've been through."

Dean pressed a kiss to the top of her head. "Sweetheart, it all fades away when I look at you."

"But you have to be so angry, and you have every right."

"Dwelling on all of that will only make us crazy. How about we just take up from here and go on? I can't make you three or six or twelve again, Grace, much as I'd dearly love to go through every single day with you." He stopped, turned her to him, grasping her shoulders. "But everything I know of you makes me happy as I can be to think I can go through the rest of my years with you back in my life. Linda did a terrible thing taking you from us, but—" his voice cracked "—looks to me like she did right by you. She was good to you, Grace?"

She nodded, unable to speak.

"Then I owe her for that. Owe Dan Hunt, too—he's a good man."

"He is, and I—" Her heart was thudding as she forced herself to broach the topic that haunted her. "I have a daddy. I don't want to hurt you, but I can't just walk away from him. He's been my rock. I'm sorry." She touched his arm. "I'm sorry because that hurts you."

"I could get real mad at life or fate or whatever for taking you away from me." His gaze locked on hers. "But what good would that do any of us?" He thought a minute, then shook his head. "We can't focus on that." His shoulders rose as he took a deep breath. "I'll never ask you to quit loving the man who raised you, sweetheart. I will ask you to give me a chance to earn your love, too. What you call me isn't nearly as important as never losing you again. Whatever you need me to do in order to be part of your life, that's what I'll do. And I'm pretty sure I speak for all of us."

She studied this man, so obviously in pain yet generous and kind, nonetheless. How hard must it be to know that another man had been through all the precious moments, that your child called someone else Daddy? "Would it be okay if I called you Papa?"

"It would be—" He choked up and had to try again. "I would be honored."

Grace let herself feel the love pouring off this man in waves and for the first time since a bombshell had been dropped into her life, hope stole in, replacing grief. Instead of what she was losing, she could glimpse what she had to gain, and her heart, so battered and frightened, began to ease. She drew back a little, wiping her eyes. "Should we go inside or would it be better if I waited for another day?"

"Oh, sweetheart, we've waited too long already. Please—"

He gestured, keeping one arm around her shoulders. "Welcome home, daughter."

They began to walk toward the front door, but before they reached the porch, the door opened and her birth family streamed outside.

"YOU'RE PACING," observed Jared. "Does it help?"

Garrett shot him a dark look. "What do you think?"

"Not so much. You've got it bad for my sister, don't you?" He held up a hand. "And before you say she's not my sister, think again."

"I wouldn't say that, anyway. She needs you. The Grossos are the ones she's not sure she wants." Garrett smacked one fist into the other palm. "Damn it, I should be there with her. She didn't have to go alone."

"Welcome to our world. It's who she is."

"Then how can we ever make a life together?" Garrett demanded. "If she rejects me when the chips are down?"

"Whoa, dude. This isn't about you. Grace is the one who takes care of people, not the one who leans. If you can't accept who she is, then just move on."

Garrett whirled on him. "I'm not going anywhere, get that through your head. Just because she's stubborn as sin doesn't mean I'm giving up. She keeps thinking I don't know what I'm getting into, but she's wrong."

Jared looked out the front window, where Ethan's daughter, Sadie, was playing with Millie and Bella while Ethan kicked a soccer ball with Matthew. "Three kids is a lot to take on." His glance at Garrett was filled with speculation. "You've been footloose for a long time."

"I didn't have Grace then."

"You better be sure, Garrett. Don't you mess with her heart."

He turned to Jared. "Look, I know my reputation better than any of you, but there was no reason before to do anything but live large. I never expected Grace, never understood before what it could be like to have someone make your world so…right. So solid and real. She's sexy as hell, and I'll die wanting to make love to her, but—"

Jared winced. "TMI, bud."

Garrett grinned but soon grew serious again. "But there's so much more to her. She's funny and bright and warm…so warm when I never realized my world was cold. Look, I know she could do better than me—what do I know about a solid family, after all? But I see her and watch how you all are together, and I can't tell you I won't make mistakes, but I can promise that I'll spend my life trying to deserve her. And I love those kids already."

"Sounds pretty good to me, son." Garrett hadn't heard Dan approach from behind, but Dan clapped a hand on his shoulder. "So how about you and your brother cut this guy some slack, Jared? Grace is a grown woman, and she knows her own mind."

"But she's under a lot of pressure," Jared protested. "Maybe she's not thinking right."

For a second, Garrett considered the idea that what had passed between him and Grace might be an illusion, and the pain that tore through him robbed him of breath.

"No." He turned on her brother. That very anguish was proof that what he felt for her was real, and damn it, she hadn't been lying when she said she loved him, had she? "You're wrong."

She'd leaned on him.

He wasn't giving up without a fight.

He wasn't leaving her to face this all alone, either. "I have an idea. Grace is worried about having to give up one family to accept another. How about if we prove her wrong?"

"What's your plan?" Dan asked.

Relieved to be acting instead of waiting, Garrett began to explain.

"WILL YOU TEACH ME HOW YOU make those pecan tassies?" Juliana asked.

Grace blinked. "*Me* teach *you?* When everyone knows

you're the best cook in NASCAR?" After she'd been held and hugged and cried over, passed from one person to the next, Juliana and Patsy had led her into the big kitchen, seeming to understand that she needed a little reprieve from all the emotion charging the atmosphere.

Patsy stood beside her like a sentinel, every once in a while simply touching her arm, her hand, her shoulder as if she might disappear. "She's got competition now, I think. You're pretty amazing yourself."

"Oh, no, I—" Grace was flustered.

"Will you let me feed you?" Juliana asked. "Will you share the meal with us?"

"I…" It was all so much to deal with. "My kids are home from school by now, and I always like to hear about their day and give them a snack. I was gone a lot last week."

"You're a good mama." Juliana beamed. "This I'm sure of."

"Thank you. I want to be—" She halted. "What should I call you?"

"Your brother and sister call me Nana."

Brother and sister. It was still like a dream. Kent had clasped her shoulders and stared at her, obviously trying, as she had, to see the resemblance of twins. "Sophia looks a little like me, doesn't she?"

Patsy's eyes swam. "She looks more your twin than Kent does."

"He's so tall. And very handsome," Grace hastened to add.

"As is your Garrett," Juliana noted, eagle eyes sharpening. "He is yours, is he not?" She grinned. "We saw you at his car, as did most of America."

"I don't know what we are yet. I mean, he says he loves me, but—" She placed a hand on her stomach. "He's going to be very unhappy that I came here without him."

"He's a good boy," said Juliana. "We are all quite fond of him."

"I should go see him. He's worried."

A cryptic smile played over Patsy's lips. "I think he'll be all right. Please stay a little longer, will you?"

Grace frowned, uneasy about any more delays. "I'd better not, but I'll come back, maybe tomorrow."

"We would like you to come anytime you're willing. Every day," Juliana said. "This is your home now."

Grace couldn't figure out how to explain that it wasn't home yet, though the welcome she'd received had warmed her. Before she could, the swinging door to the kitchen opened.

"Mommy!" Bella charged across the floor.

"What are you doing here?"

"Garrett and Grandpop said we have more family to love us. Did you know there are horses here? And some cows." As a bewildered Grace automatically lifted Bella into her arms, Bella glanced at Patsy. "Are they your horses? Can I ride one?"

"May I, young lady," said Grace. "And we don't ask, we wait to be offered."

Bella encompassed Patsy and Juliana with an angelic smile. "Grandpop says you're very nice. That maybe you might let me."

More family to love them. A nice sentiment, but exactly what had Garrett and Daddy said to the kids? Right now, however, there were manners to be discussed. "Grandpop said that, or you decided on your own that they might let you?"

All innocence, Bella smiled again. "They might."

Laughter filled the room, some of it male.

"If your mom is all right with it, I have just the pony for you to try," Dean offered.

Grace turned to see Dean with Dan right behind him, Millie in Dan's arms, Milo following them. "Where's Matthew?"

"Right here." Garrett stepped past them, his hand on Matthew's shoulder. Jared, Ethan and Hope followed. "We're all here for you, right where we should be." No anger, only love shone from his eyes.

Deep inside her, a long-wound tension eased.

As she glanced around the room, she saw fathers and brothers and sisters, grandparents and mothers and children, some bound by blood and others tied together by the heart, every person seemingly united by one thing: that they cared about her.

Grace realized in that moment that she wasn't lost, after all, but found. Not bereft, not stranded, not alone unless she made herself that way.

She was loved. Most people had only one family, but she was blessed to have two. It didn't have to be complicated. As her gaze blurred, she felt her children surround her as Garrett crossed the room and took her in his arms.

"You're home, Grace," he murmured. Then, to her astonishment, he stepped back and went to one knee. "I figure that here, surrounded by everyone who loves you, is a better place than the fancy meal I had planned to ask if you'll let me make a home with you." He pulled a small box from his pocket and opened it.

Bella gasped before he could speak. "Look, Mommy, Garrett wants to marry us! I told you he would!"

Grace looked from one child to the next, seeing the hope in their eyes.

"Will you marry me, all of you?" Garrett asked Grace and her children somberly.

Matthew glanced up at her. "Want to, Mom?"

"I do. How about you?"

He nodded.

"Millie?"

"Yes," she said softly, slipping over to stand beside Garrett.

Grace looked at her wiggly four-year-old. "I bet I know your answer."

"He's really pretty, Mommy."

Laughter rocketed around the room, and Grace was amused to see Garrett's cheeks flush with color. Her gaze scanned the assembled group, seeing her joy mirrored on all their faces.

At last it landed on him, Garrett Clark, the playboy she

would never in a million years have expected to become the love of her life. "He is," she agreed. She extended her left hand, surprised it wasn't shaking as hard as her knees. "Thank you," she said to Garrett, to everyone in the room, to fate and the forces of good. "We would be honored to marry you."

Garrett slipped the ring on her finger and rose to kiss her tenderly while Patsy diplomatically plucked Bella from her arms.

"You're pretty, too" she heard Bella saying to the woman Bella and Millie and Matthew would grow up to know as their grandmother.

Grace smiled against Garrett's lips. "Thank you for bringing everyone here," she whispered.

"Wouldn't be anywhere else," he murmured as he held her close.

Then he turned and gestured to all the smiling faces.

"Welcome home, Grace."

* * * * *

*A sample from THE MEMORY OF A KISS
by Wendy Etherington and Abby Gaines,
the first book in the next NASCAR series...*

DANE WAS CONTENT talking about drafting, tires and straight-away speeds. These were things he expected.

"Hello, gorgeous."

That voice, however, was unexpected.

He hadn't heard that voice live in more than fourteen years. He'd sat in many dark rooms, wondered about the past and the present, and let her words, recorded in high-tech digital sound, soothe his soul. The continued weakness after so much pain was a part of him he both resented and would never admit.

Bracing himself, he turned to face Lizzie Lancaster.

With her tall, slender body, fiery hair and deep ocean-blue eyes, she was as stunning as her pictures, different than he remembered in person. She lit up the room and stood out clearly as a superstar. Even in the presence of several.

Before he could say a word, she pulled him into a tight hug, brushing her lips over his cheek as she leaned back. "It's been a long time."

The scent of her exotic-smelling perfume and the warmth of her mouth lingered even after they were no longer touching. His stomach clenched.

"Yeah," he managed to say, clearly recalling the rainy spring afternoon he'd watched her climb on a bus and roll out of town and out of his life.

What was she doing here?

Watching the girl he used to love—the one he'd thought he'd

spend his life with—as she flirted, chatted and drew every eye in the room was physically painful. She'd made him vulnerable to that pain. A weakness he'd sworn he'd never feel again.

Dane gripped his beer bottle and fought the impulse to run.

*Harlequin Intrigue top author Delores Fossen presents
a brand-new series of breathtaking romantic suspense!*
TEXAS MATERNITY: HOSTAGES
The first installment available May 2010:
THE BABY'S GUARDIAN

Shaw cursed and hooked his arm around Sabrina.

Despite the urgency that the deadly gunfire created, he tried to be careful with her, and he took the brunt of the fall when he pulled her to the ground. His shoulder hit hard, but he held on tight to his gun so that it wouldn't be jarred from his hand.

Shaw didn't stop there. He crawled over Sabrina, sheltering her pregnant belly with his body, and he came up ready to return fire.

This was obviously a situation he'd wanted to avoid at all cost. He didn't want his baby in the middle of a fight with these armed fugitives, but when they fired that shot, they'd left him no choice. Now, the trick was to get Sabrina safely out of there.

"Get down," someone on the SWAT team yelled from the roof of the adjacent building.

Shaw did. He dropped lower, covering Sabrina as best he could.

There was another shot, but this one came from a rifleman on the SWAT team. Shaw didn't look up, but he heard the sound of glass being blown apart.

The shots continued, all coming from his men, which meant it might be time to try to get Sabrina to better cover. Shaw glanced at the front of the building.

So that Sabrina's pregnant belly wouldn't be smashed against the ground, Shaw eased off her and moved her to a sitting position so that her back was against the brick wall. They were close. Too close. And face-to-face.

He found himself staring right into those sea-green eyes.

How will Shaw get Sabrina out?
Follow the daring rescue and the heartbreaking
aftermath in THE BABY'S GUARDIAN by Delores Fossen,
available May 2010 from Harlequin Intrigue.